ALL ROADS LE.

BY: Alora Tefariah

<u>PROLOUGE</u>

How much is your soul worth? Have you ever asked yourself what amount of money it would take to get you to do something you never thought you'd do? Something so repulsive and embarrassing that you have to bury it deep inside in order to go on in life? I was only 21 and found myself asking the same question. It was no secret that I loved money and a lavish lifestyle, anyone on the outside looking in would trade places with me in a New York minute based off what I allowed them to see. Scrolling through my social media you'd envy me. I'm every man's fantasy and my beauty makes even the most confident girls second guess themselves. I'd recently been dating one of the hottest rappers in the game, and I'd even been on a few blogs because of it. I was living the lavish life according to my Instagram posts, driving a Mercedes and living in my own high rise, being flown all around the world, experiencing things only a few people get to see in their life time.

I'd been dating the mainstream rapper, we will call Lil Saint, for about seven months and he'd flown me all across the world to ensure I'd be available to him in each city during his tour. Although the blogs had captured us leaving the Hyde hotel in Miami and were quick to run the story of me being his girlfriend; what they didn't capture were the three random women he'd brought back from the tour bus and made me have sex with.

Yeah, America's favorite rapper was into some freaky orgy type shit. But he was fucking Lil Saint! I mean to me all the gifts, trips, money spent and jewelry were enough for me to do pretty much anything he requested in the bedroom, or on the yacht, or on a balcony of a penthouse, shit pretty much anywhere he wanted it I was down and willing. For seven months I got to taste the good life. I got to see what it was like to live in the spotlight and I was hooked.

So, you can imagine the disappointment when I'd gotten back from, what was supposed to be a lit birthday weekend celebration in Vegas with Lil Saint, only to find that he'd changed his number and blocked me on all social media. I was devastated, hurt, angry and all of those things. But most of all I was confused as I sat on the living room floor of my downtown apartment dialing his number over and over again as if the "The number you have called is not a working number. Please hang up and try your call again." message was going to change.

The tears were just beginning to fall from my eyes as my phone rang. My anxiety was getting the best of me because without even looking at the caller ID I answered, "Saint what the hell is going on?" I asked as I sniffled to prevent my nose from running. "Bitch have you been on Facebook?" I heard my best friend Latasha scream into the phone. "What? What are you talking about, why?"

"Bitch them hoes done put out some list that claims you slept with half the niggas in Atlanta."

"WHAT?! What hoes? What are you talking about?" I was genuinely confused as to what or who she was referring to. On top of that I was still dealing with all my thoughts on Lil Saint. "Bitch get on Facebook, Chanel and them done made a post that has gone viral with your pictures all on it."

You see where I'm from, St. Louis Missouri, it was very small and everyone knew each other so gossip spread fast. When the Lil Saint story hit the blogs, I started getting hate from all directions even from family and those I considered friends.

There weren't many success stories coming out of St. Louis; and don't get it twisted, mine isn't either. I'll start with the back story with how I ended up in Atlanta in the first place, it's going to be a lot to take in so sit back and grab your popcorn, it's about to be one hell of a show.

CHAPTER ONE

I'd graduated high school one month prior and I knew that college wasn't going to be the route for me early on. My parents, Meshaun and Melvin Simmons, had made it clear that if I was going to stay in their house, I had to either go to college or get a job so I was working at the mall in one of the hottest shoe stores inside. I made over $1,000 a week in commission alone and on top of my $12.50 an hour check I was doing very well in my eyes at 18 with a car that was paid for aside from the $200 a month I was giving my parents I didn't have any other bills.

My best friend Latasha was 6 months pregnant with her son and we couldn't really hang like we used to. So, it didn't bother me that the store was short staffed and had asked me to come in on a Saturday. While working; a group of girls filed into the store speaking loudly about a party they were going to that evening. The loudest, the one who seemed to lead the other girls, was a short brown skin girl with brown eyes and 40" blonde hair extensions. I could tell she was probably the girlfriend of a rapper or drug dealer and the crew was most definitely not from St. Louis. "Good afternoon ladies are you all looking for anything in particular?" I asked as I made my way in front of the group; mind on the sales. "Yeah, Princess is it?" She asked as she read my name tag. "Yes?"

"I'm looking for 5 pair of them new air maxes that just dropped, I'm a size 7 everyone else gotta tell you their size." She said as she began to walk past me and look at some of the sweatsuits on the rack behind me. I got the other girl's sizes before going to the back praying that we had all 5 pair. To my surprise we did so I brought them all to the front and the blonde one stated, "Nah we don't need to try them on take them to the register."

While ringing them up the blonde one struck up a conversation by complimenting me. "Damn I didn't realize how pretty you were, look at them freckles and you got the nerve to have some green eyes! What you mixed with?" She asked with a laugh. "Oh, I'm not mixed both my parents are black." I answered proudly, "Would you like each box in separate bags?" I asked; quickly trying to change the subject. "Yeah, that's cool. So, Princess what you doing tonight? You trying to party at the Spotlight? My man got me a section so everything already paid for and if you need an outfit, I can get you something." She said as she handed me her credit card to pay her $1300 bill.

"I mean I don't get off until nine." I answered reluctantly. I really wanted to go because the entire city was talking about Nelly's birthday party. I had just celebrated my 18th birthday and the club was 21 and up so I was trying to figure out how I was going to pull this one off. "That's cool we not rolling out until about 11:30 anyway. here." She said pulling a pen and small notebook out of her purse before jotting her number on it and handing it to me. "Call me, I'll scoop you up. And don't worry you won't need ID with me." She assured me before her and her crew turned to make their exit, stopping abruptly she turned back around before saying, "By the way, when people ask you, always tell them you're mixed. It makes you more mysterious and a whole lot sexier." She winked before walking away to join her crew outside the store. "Wait, I didn't catch your name." I called out behind her as they began to make their exit. "Chanel, make sure you call me!"

That night when I got off, I was sitting in the parking lot contemplating on calling the girl. I mean I was trying to party but I didn't know her from a can of paint. "Fuck it." I said to myself as I dialed her number. She answered on the second ring, "Who is this?"

"Hey I'm looking for Chanel, this Princess from Shoe Locker." I responded hesitantly. "Oh, what's up girl? I didn't think you were gonna call. Where you at?"

"I'm just now getting to my car about to head home to get dressed."

"Nah scratch that; go home and grab you something for tonight and to sleep in, I'll text you the address to my hotel and the room number. I have a whole crew of MUA's and hair stylist to get you right. Try to hurry we heading out in about two and a half hours but what's a party without the pre-game?" She insisted; and before I could argue she ended the call with, "Ok sending the addy now. See you soon!"

I can't lie Chanel seemed to be such an "IT" girl. She walked like she was six feet tall, however, her petite frame only stood at about 5'4". Her presence could be felt when she entered a room. She knew she was that bitch and I was intrigued. I didn't really hang with the party girls in high school because my father was very strict but the closer I got to 21 the more I wanted to explore the night life.

I got to my house and began throwing all my

shower shit in a bag before opening my closet door and trying to decide which of the 3 black dresses I owned would be the attire for the night. One was the black dress I had to wear to my grand pops funeral, another was the dress I wore under my graduation gown and the third was a graduation gift from one of my 3 older brothers, MJ, who was a 21-year-old designer in his senior year of college. It was obvious his creation was the best choice, at least it was kind of sexy. I grabbed a pair of heels, which I collected so I had literally hundreds of them, and made my way back out to my car. I typed the address into the GPS and was relieved that the hotel was only 12 minutes from my house.

Once I parked at the hotel, I made my way up to Chanel's room which, not surprisingly, was a suite on the very top floor. A tall guy dressed in all black opened the room door for me and announced my presence before I saw Chanel pop her head out from a doorway. "Hey you made it! We in here getting our makeup done, put your bags down and come on in here." She grabbed my hand and I sat my bags down; following her lead. We walked into a bedroom that was the size of some people's apartments.

It was decorated in all cream and gold with a triple king California king rise bed in the center of the room that was framed in an all-gold bed frame and headboard. She walked us to the bathroom inside of the room that was pretty big too. There was music playing and the same girls that was with her at the mall, with addition of three MUAs that were busy working on three of the girls faces.

"So, you from here?" She asked me as I took a seat on the side of the jacuzzi tub. "Unfortunately." I admitted as Chanel handed me a red plastic cup filled with alcohol. "You ever been to Atlanta?"

"Not yet, always wanted to though."

"When we leave here tomorrow afternoon that's where we headed, you tryna slide?" She looked at me as if she were studying my face; but I didn't hesitate when I responded, "Hell yeah!" I figured my life needed some type of adventure and I was tired of St. Louis I was bigger than the Lou. "Ok then it's settled, I'll get your ticket now and we can go shopping before we head out."

"Shit I'd rather go shopping in Atlanta! I want some shit these hoes up here don't have."

"That's even better!" She agreed before lighting up a blunt and taking out her phone to take pictures of herself. "What's your Instagram name?" Chanel asked as she began typing the caption for her picture. "Oh, I'm not really on social media like that. I just have a Facebook." I admitted a little embarrassed. "What?" All the girls stated more so than asked in unison before we all shared a laugh. "Yeah, I just never caught that wave."

"Well, we are about to change that. Let me see your phone." Chanel stood in front of me handing me the blunt as I passed her my phone. "Ok I'm gonna create you a page, what do you want your name to be?"

"I can't just use princess?" It was my turn to get my makeup done as I exhaled the smoke and passed the blunt back to Chanel. "No, you don't have a nickname?" Chanel asked, still in my phone creating my page. "I mean my mom calls me Moon; long story doesn't ask." I said with a laugh. "Hmmm, maybe I can work with that."

Chanel went to work in my phone creating me a profile under the name @LickMyMoonPie while the MUA continued to work her magic. "Y'all done turned down, it's time to make a toast before we turn this bitch back up. She raised her cup as all the other girls did the same, "To one hell of a night."

"To one hell of a night!" We all said in unison before we all drank from our glasses.

CHAPTER TWO

After I met Chanel, I found myself loving the lifestyle she was allotted due to who she was involved with. Now her boyfriend was married at the time so we will call him "King"; and King was definitely paid! King was giving her a monthly allowance, he paid for her travel, clothes, bills and pretty much anything she asked for he'd pay for. He'd even bought her a condo in Buckhead and a Range Rover. He was in love with Chanel but he made it very clear that he would never leave his wife for her, and she was ok with that.

Chanel taught me how to spot a nigga with money a mile away and she taught me how to talk to them in order to benefit from them. She always reminded me that the goal was to date for money not love so all that "I have to be attracted to him." went out the window for me. She taught me how to dress and how to allow my presence to be felt before I was even seen. I can't lie, Chanel had turned me into a "Bad Bitch" and I was no longer the shy shoe girl she'd met two years prior.

In just two years Chanel had upgraded my way of thinking and my lifestyle. I finally understood the power of social media as I had reached over 200K followers and the attention of a different caliber of men whom otherwise I would've never even been able to be in the presence of. I'd been out on dates with some ball players, rappers and singers but none on the level of King.

However, I was able to get them to pay to send me to hair and makeup school and one ball player I dated got my first high rise apartment in midtown for me. One of my suiters filled the spot with brand new furniture while one of them had gotten me a brand-new Mercedes. I was so ready for one of them to wife me but I hadn't gotten so lucky yet.

Chanel and I were in a hotel room out in Vegas that year and there were a few other men in the suite along with about three or four other girls that we didn't know. I was vibing with a guy who happened to be an engineer for a huge record company, he had a nice vibe even though he was a white boy. We were all drinking and eating good lobster tails, crab legs, caviar, corn and potatoes when the door to the suite burst open and in stormed Queen, King's wife, along with two other females.

Queen was a beautiful woman in her mid-30's who was also the mother of their four-year-old daughter. Her jet-black hair was up in a sloppy bun and from the way she was dressed I could tell she did not come to talk. The entire suite fell silent as she stormed past everyone and into the main room of the suite. I could hear a scream and security ran into the room as I followed close behind. I made it to the doorway and was stopped abruptly by the security as I watched helplessly as Queen's friends jumped Chanel who was naked from the waist down.

King finally got security to break up the fight and quickly went into PR mode as he directed security that no one was to leave without signing an NDA to never speak of the incident again. Chanel had retreated to the bathroom and locked herself inside while Queen and her friends angrily left the suite, being followed by security. The look on Queen's face was true heartbreak. She had tears in her eyes but I never saw one fall as she and her friends made their way out back out of the suite. After a few minutes I finally got security to let me in the room to try to talk to Chanel.

I knocked on the bathroom door, "Chanel it's me unlock the door." After a brief silence I heard the door click and she let me inside. "Girl, what the fuck? How the hell she know where y'all were at?" I asked her as I examined her face. Surprisingly she didn't have any signs of having just been jumped outside of the small red mark on her cheek. "Bitch cause she stalking me on social media. How you have two bitches jump me and still left a bitch sitting on pretty." Chanel laughed as she fixed her lace front.

"Bitch you so damn crazy, I tried to help you but security swarmed me."

"I ain't tripping, King not letting nothing happen to that crazy bitch. Just like he not gone let this crazy pussy walk out his life. That bitch just gone make me suck his dick harder tonight. She don't even know she just got me a new truck!" She burst into laughter as she refreshed her lipstick. I couldn't help but laugh as she brushed past me, placing her hand on the door knob, she turned her head back and winked, "Watch this." She whispered before opening the door.

King was seated on the end of the bed with his phone in his hand, noticeably frustrated, while the other hand rested on his head. "Daddy look what they did to my face." Chanel said in her soft baby voice as he looked up at her. I was a little baffled that he hadn't followed his wife but I just stood there watching his demeanor soften when he looked in Chanel's eyes. The craziest part of witnessing this was the fact that King and Queen were literally "relationship goals" on all the blogs and magazines. They'd been married for years and both had successful careers in the entertainment industry, hence why I can't tell you their real names and have changed some of their physical attributes to stay safe. But the way he looked at Chanel I knew his heart belonged to her. It was no doubt that he was in fact in love with two women.

After throwing his phone behind him on the bed he pulled Chanel down on his lap and kissed her bruised cheek. "You know her ass crazy baby but what can I do to make it up to you?" he grabbed her chin and began kissing her hard. For some reason I couldn't pull my eyes away. I'd always been attracted to King long before I ever met him or Chanel and I was feeling my heartbeat between my legs as he twisted his hand in her hair and gently guided her down into his lap. Chanel didn't hesitate as she pulled his dick out of his robe and devouring him whole. He kept his hand in her hair as the security closed the bedroom door;

leaving me standing there as she gave him head.

"You just gone stand there and watch or you gone get some of this big hard dick too?" King said to me as he patted the bed next to him. The Patron I'd been drinking all night along with the fact that King was fine as fuck had me sashaying my sexy ass right on over to where they were. I instantly took advantage of the opportunity to kiss one of the richest rappers in the world. I licked on his ear before sticking my tongue in his mouth and enjoying his hand around my neck. "Strip." He demanded as he abruptly ended our kiss. I stood back up from the bed and began to take my clothes off slowly.

He pulled on Chanel's hair and she came up for air, "Give her some of that tongue for me." He told her before she got off her knees and came over to me. Chanel got right into it as she snatched my hair back and bit my neck gently. "Bring yo sexy ass over here, I'm about to snatch your soul." She smacked my ass and King got up and walked over to the dresser in the room to roll up a backwoods. My pussy was throbbing and juicy when I got on the bed. "No, stay just like that." Chanel instructed me to stay in the doggy style position before getting on the bed behind me placing soft kisses on my ass as she stuck two fingers inside of me.

I moaned out in pleasure as I stared over at King seductively. I can't lie I was trying to do some Jedi mind trick shit to get that nigga to beg Chanel to bring me in on their agreement. Hell, I didn't give a fuck. He was muthafuckin King! He was standing with his Versace robe open and his hard dick was at full attention as he watched Chanel pleasure me. The next thing I knew Chanel's soft kisses turned to her tongue swirling on thighs before sliding her warm tongue over my wet slit before landing in my asshole. At first, I jumped a bit so Chanel taunted me, "Oh nah don't run! I told you I'm about to snatch your soul lil sexy bitch."

I had never had my salad tossed but that shit started feeling good as fuck and before I knew it, I was shaking as I began to climax. King had sparked the blunt and made his way over to the bed. He stood in front of me and without a word I took him whole into my mouth as I massaged his balls with my hands. I was giving him everything I had as I continued to get pleased from behind by Chanel.

That next day when I awakened King was

already gone and Chanel was asleep with her head on my stomach. I had a spinning headache and my mouth was dry as fuck. I slowly moved Chanel's head as I inched out the bed to find my clothes. I couldn't believe that Chanel and I had crossed that line but shit I got to fuck King and that shit was good as fuck! I couldn't help but smile as the memories from the night before rushed through my mind. I pleased myself in the shower from the thought of it alone.

CHAPTER THREE

The following day King had a private car service pick us up from the airport in Atlanta and take us to a car dealership. My mind was absolutely blown when I found out that he upgraded Chanel's truck to a new Range Rover. She drove it right off the lot, in her name and paid for! I couldn't believe how easily men would come out their pockets to protect their dirty secrets.

You see most people don't understand why these celebrity men or men of a certain stature are willing to spend thousands of dollars on women who they wouldn't marry. But in the short time I'd known and watched Chanel operate I quickly learned the reason. These men are paying for everything their wives aren't willing to do. Simple. Some of these men were into the freakiest of the freak and they could afford the price tag.

One of the common misconceptions is that we slept with all of our suiters or tricks, which isn't the case. Take me for instance; one of my suiters at the time was a man that paid me $3,000 a month just for my period panties. Then there was Walter, my suiter with a crazy foot fetish that paid me $1000 every time we linked just to smash bread on his chest with my feet. Oh, and let me not forget George, he was my oldest suiter being 64 but he paid me for my company. His wife of 30 years had passed away two years prior and he would pay me $1,300 a month to come have dinner with him in his wife's clothes and wigs. You see in Atlanta these types of men are everywhere, and like Chanel, there wasn't much I wouldn't do for money.

After the Vegas trip King was added to my list of suiters. He'd given me $10,000 before we left Vegas and that was the most money, I'd gotten out of a man at one time so I was hooked. He could ask me to do damn near anything and guess what? A bitch was gone do it! Chanel didn't seem to mind especially because it was clear that King would never stop messing with her. In fact; Chanel and I were even closer after we began messing around. The time following the Vegas trip we were inseparable. At first it was only for King but then we started messing around on the regular just the two of us.

One day after we'd been out shopping all day, we decided to go to a spa by the name of Jeju about an hour outside the city. Once we were inside Chanel and I signed up for almost all of the packages and were enjoying one of the saunas when two young women walked in and joined us. Being the type of female Chanel is I wasn't surprised when she sparked up convo with the beautiful women.

"What do y'all do?" Chanel asked the lighter skin one from the duo. "We are models, y'all got Instagram? Follow us, y'all look like the type of chicks I'm trying to kick shit with." She said with a laugh. "Shoot what y'all doing this weekend? My man got us a fat ass suite in Miami if y'all down to slide." Chanel offered. The two looked at each other but didn't take long to agree to the trip. King had a show in Miami and he wanted Chanel and I close so he'd gotten the room in his favorite hotel for the weekend for us to stay in. We exchanged numbers with the ladies before making plans to link the following night at a local night club.

The next night, as promised, we were all dressed up and smelling good as we pulled up to the Gold Room. The city was on fire per usual and this particular night Diddy and his star-studded guest list was in the building. We pulled up to the valet and were escorted right through the front door to our pre-paid section. The bottles were popped and we were vibing to the DJ's set when the two ladies, Shanell and Farrah, finally joined us.

They were both dressed in the latest designer and dripping in diamonds. These girls were definitely my type of chicks. Farrah walked right up and gave us both hugs but Shanell pretended to be preoccupied with her phone. "I'm ready to turn up! Y'all look bomb as fuck!" Farrah complimented as she picked the bottle up off the table and poured it into her open mouth.

As the night went on Shanell ended up loosening up and we actually all had a great time together as if we'd been friends for years. When it was time to leave, we all decided to go to a restaurant to grab something to eat before heading home. It wasn't until we were seated when the conversation actually got interesting. "So, what do y'all do? Y'all stuntin' in Gold Room in a playa ass section wit no niggas I know y'all gotta be paid." Farrah wasn't shy at all as she sipped on her bottled water through a straw.

"We basically get paid off of IG, we're both Instagram models so people pay us to promote and shit like that." Chanel quickly answered. "What is it that you ladies do? I can tell y'all got a lil paper too." Chanel added. "Well, Shanell has a rich step father and Nigerian boyfriend and me; well, I basically date rich white men for money." She said with a laugh. "You mean like an escort?" I asked, not able to help myself. "Basically. But shit it's good money, I travel for free and it comes with all kinds of other perks." Farrah was African American and Indian but her Indian features were more dominant. She had long thick black hair to the middle of her back, thick eyebrows, almond eyes and olive skin. She was definitely a foreign beauty that men were willing to pay for.

At the restaurant Farrah told us all about a company that she worked for that handled her "dates". The money she was making was crazy and it was something that I could do without switching up my lifestyle. I made sure that I got her number for myself before we parted ways that night. On the way home Chanel made it clear that what Farrah was doing was out of the question for the type of bitch she was training me to be, and just like that the thought became just a fantasy as Chanel made me delete Farrah's number from my phone in front of her.

When we got back to my crib Chanel came inside with me and sat on my couch as I went in the kitchen to get us some wine and put up my food from the restaurant. When I came back in the living room Chanel was on facetime with King and she was smiling from ear to ear. "Hey daddy we just got back to Princess crib from Gold Room. How was your show tonight?" She asked him as I sat next to her and handed her the glass of wine. "It was off the chain you already know I killed that shit. We just left this strip club out here about to take it back to the room. How my other baby doing? Stand up so I can see how y'all was representing me tonight." He demanded and we both, without hesitation, stood to our feet and allowed King to examine us.

"Damn y'all looking good as a muthafuckin, let me see something so daddy can sleep good tonight." King instructed Chanel who didn't ask any questions before pulling me close to her and sticking her tongue in and out of my mouth, causing me to moan enticingly. "Sit the phone on the tripod I bought you so I can see what I been missing." Chanel and I were giggling at nothing in particular as we made our way to my bedroom. As she set the phone up on the tripod I began to undress. By the time she joined me on the bed I was topless and wearing only my laced black panties. She pulled a small vile from in-between her breasts and instructed me to turn over before she slid it across my ass while it dispensed a line of cocaine. She proceeded to snort the line off my ass before removing my panties with her teeth.

King continued to give her directions of what he wanted to see as she pleased me from behind, she took her finger and placed a small amount of coke on it before inserting it inside my asshole before grabbing one of my dildos and stuffing it inside my wet vagina. That shit drove me insane the way the coke would make her touch feel as I imagined it was King entering me with his thick manhood. It didn't take me long to explode all over the dildo and then it was my turn to return the favor.

Before meeting Chanel, I had never even looked at a female in a sexual manner but my attraction to her lifestyle and her man had me willing to do damn near anything if it meant keeping my position in their lives and bedroom. I was a pro at giving her head at this point so it didn't take me long to make her squirt as King watched on from the camera. I flicked my tongue over her clit feverishly as she grabbed at the back of my head. I gently guided two fingers in and out as I watched her cum again for us. I came up and smiled as I stuck my fingers in her mouth before kissing her.

King was in love with Chanel but he loved the way I was submissive to him and obedient to his commands; no matter what they were. I made his dick hard with my presence alone and I loved it. What Chanel didn't know was that he and I had exchanged numbers in Vegas and we were communicating on the regular outside of her. I wasn't trying to steal him from her or anything I just wanted him to fall for me too since we were already sharing him.

King got a business call and ended the call so Chanel and I hopped in the shower before laying in the bed to call it a night. The next day when we woke up, we had to immediately get ready to head to the airport to head to Miami. The plane ride wasn't even two hours long but when we got to Miami it was pouring down raining when we arrived to the hotel. After checking in we made our way to the top floor to our suite and settled in a bit before we facetimed King.

His show was at 10 that night so we had a few hours to kill since our flight got us there at 4.

We decided to go grab something to eat from the restaurant downstairs and took a seat at the bar. While waiting for our drinks and having casual conversation two guys came and sat at the bar next to us. They were both attractive and visibly paid. The one seated closest to me asked us what we were drinking when our drinks arrived and after answering he instructed to put anything we ordered on his tab.

"I didn't catch you ladies name." He stated, looking in our direction. "I'm Moon and this is my girl Ch-"

"Chante'." Chanel quickly cut me off. "I'm Issac and this is my business associate and good friend Qwami. You ladies look beautiful are you from around here or just visiting?"

"We are just visiting, what business are you gentlemen in?" Chanel asked as she sipped from the lemon drop that'd been placed in front of her. "I'm an investor and day trader and my boy here is in sports management. Are you ladies free tonight by chance?"

"We're never free, everything over here expensive." Chanel answered as she stared in his eyes to watch for his response. "Oh, is that right?

So, what expenses you need paid Moon?" He directed his response towards me and I smiled because he was more of my type than his friend was. "All of them." I responded with a wink. He and his friend both laughed before he continued, "Ok well I'm sure I can afford it. Take my number down."

After we finished eating and drinking, we made our way back upstairs to get dressed for the night. I was especially excited because I couldn't wait to see King. I knew he was Chanel's man but my body craved him just as much. "Which one do you think I should rock? The lime green or the yellow mufukka?" Chanel was standing in the doorway of my bathroom butt ass naked holding up the two dress options for the night. "What shoes you wearing?" I asked as I applied my mascara. "Bitch just tell me which dress you like better!" Chanel asked, annoyed. "I like that yellow joint but do a offset color for the shoe like a red or something." Chanel sucked her teeth and walked off without responding.

We were both dressed to kill as we walked inside the packed club and were escorted to our section. To our surprise when King finally walked in the building an hour later his wife was glued to his arm. Apparently, she'd decided she was tired of her husband's antics and decided to follow him to Miami. I looked over at Chanel who was visibly angry as she text someone from her phone. I grabbed one of the bottles off the table and poured a huge shot into my mouth.

"Let's go!" Chanel yelled over the music as she grabbed my arm. She was fuming when we jumped in the car and headed back to the hotel. The liquor I'd consumed had me feeling good and I was in no mood for her temper tantrum. "That bitch always trying to ruin some shit! Why the fuck she bring her old ass out here? She need to be home taking care of they fucking kid!" I allowed her to vent because I knew if I said anything it would be all bad. "Bitch why you over there quiet and shit?" Chanel had now put her focus on me. "Girl I'm just tipsy, fuck that bitch. Let's call the niggas from the bar earlier and see what they on!" I shrugged.

Honestly, I was just horny and ready to get some dick I really didn't care from where as long as it was attached to a deep wallet. "At this point I don't even give a fuck. Call them! But I want the nigga that said he was in investing." Chanel always found a way to try to control everything that I did but being her friend was better than not being her friend so I just dealt with it. I went ahead and dialed his number and he answered on the first ring. "Issac Hicks speaking."

"Hey Issac, this is Moon I was hoping I would catch you." I stated casually as our car pulled back up the hotel. "Moon? Wow didn't expect to hear from you tonight. What do I owe the pleasure?"

"Well, me and my girl just left the club we were just seeing what y'all were up to."

"Is that right? Well Kwame called it a night an hour ago and I'm just in my room enjoying some whiskey, you're more than welcome to join me." I covered the phone and whispered to Chanel, "Bitch his friend already sleep he's solo."

"Well tell him we both coming!" Chanel responded as we entered the lobby. "Well, if I come my girl has to as well, what room you in?"

When we made it up to his suite, he greeted us at the door with a warm smile. "You ladies looking good tonight, come on in." He stepped to the side and allowed us in before adding, "Smelling good too, y'all want me to fix y'all something to drink?" He closed the door as we walked in, both of us checking out his luxurious suite with our eyes. "What you got?" Chanel asked him as she took a seat on the couch. "I have $300 a shot whiskey." He answered with a chuckle. "That's cool I guess, so where is your friend; he sliding through?" She asked as he made his way over to the bar.

I took a seat next to Chanel on the couch and took my phone out to post for IG. "That man already done called it a night, why? What y'all on tonight?" He was making his way over to where we were seated with 3 glasses and a glass bottle filled with whiskey. "I mean we on whatever your pockets can afford." Chanel stood up and grabbed two of the glasses from him, turning to hand me one. "Is that right?" He responded with a smirk as his eyebrow raised a bit. "So, how deep are your pockets?" Chanel grabbed the glass bottle from him, popping the top, before pouring a large amount of the liquor directly into her mouth.

I knew that she was pissed about King and his wife and using this man to lash out but I didn't give a fuck. He was attractive to me and he was definitely paid! I stood up and walked over to Chanel who then poured some whiskey in my mouth before seductively kissing me and then licking on my neck. As a moan escaped my mouth Issac grabbed his rising dick and walked towards us. Chanel stopped him, gently pushing her hand into the middle of his chest. "Shit you tell me how much!" Issac was horny and we could tell he wasn't used to this type of action. "25K." Chanel didn't bat an eye as began rubbing her breasts and licking on her ear.

"Done!" His response was immediate as he pulled his phone out to begin the transfer. After we got the money, we took him out onto the patio of his suite and sat him down on one of the chairs. We'd turned some music on and were seductively dancing on one another, putting on a show for him as he sipped his whiskey and watched. I slid my hands through Chanel's hair and kissed her as I felt the liquor kick in. Issac couldn't take it anymore and he got out of the chair and joined us in a three-way kiss. We were all breathing heavy as the passion built up. We both dropped down to our knees and pulled his shorts down revealing his surprisingly large dick. I began to lick it as Chanel pulled my dress up and began playing with my pussy with one hand as she stared up into Issacs's eyes before coming down to suck his balls as I began to deep throat him, gargling a bit as I did it. Issac was brick hard as he curled his toes and held the back of my head.

He stopped me abruptly and stood both of us up, directing us to follow him. He walked us into the bedroom before demanding us to, "Get naked." We obliged and began pleasing each other on the bed while he walked over to the dresser to grab a condom. To my surprise Issac had a lot of stamina and blew our backs out until the sun came up.

The next morning, we all got into the large shower together and fucked again. He ordered us room service for breakfast and we all ate out on the balcony. There was a knock on his front door and when Issac came back from answering it, he was joined by his homeboy Kwame from the bar. "Damn it's like that?" He asked with a laugh as he recognized us. "Chill man." Issac laughed a bit before offering him excusing themselves and walking back into the suite. "If this nigga tries to fuck, we leaving." I told Chanel as I drank some of my mimosa. "Bitch if that nigga got another 25K a piece we both fucking him fuck you mean?" Chanel was posing and taking pictures for IG as the morning sun made her skin glow.

I really didn't want to fuck with the dude Kwame but Chanel was right, money talks bull shit walks. When the guys returned Kwame was cheesing from ear to ear, rubbing his hands together. "So, we were thinking that the vibe is too good to have it end here. So, what y'all day looking like? Will 50K make you both ours for the whole day?"

CHAPTER FOUR

Our last day in Miami we headed down the strip to do some shopping and sight-seeing. While leaving the Mac store we were approached by a club promoter inviting us to a party that evening hosted by one of the hottest rappers out of Atlanta at the time, we will call him Smeezy. We knew everyone would be there so it was definitely a no brainer when we accepted and Chanel took his number to put our names on the VIP list. One thing about Chanel she was not about to cry over a nigga and she damn sure wasn't missing any parties. We bar hopped for most of day before heading back to our suite to get ready for the night.

Smeezy brought out all the dope boys, scammers and other big-name celebs in the city including King. When we got in the promoter quickly took us up to the main VIP section that was on the second level and looked over the packed venue. There were several other girls around that were just as badd but one chick in particular caught my eye. Not in a sexual way but in a way that piqued my curiosity. She was about my height but way thicker than I was. She was light skin with honey brown eyes and the Coca Cola shape all men went crazy over. The long light pink lace front in her head didn't even look ghetto on her but it did make her stand out. She was wearing as many diamonds as the niggas in the section and I saw the respect she had from everyone around.

I made a mental note to find out who she was before we left that club that night. When Smeezy finally showed up the club erupted in cheer as his latest single blasted through the speakers. We danced and drank with Smeezy and his crew for the entire night and when I saw pink hair seated alone rolling up a blunt by one of the tables I knew my window of opportunity had opened. Since Chanel was preoccupied with a nigga with Smeezy crew I knew she wouldn't notice. Chanel always seemed to get jealous when I would talk to any other females outside of her even though I really didn't even look at other women in a sexual manner outside of her.

I casually made my way over to take a seat next to the girl and she wasted no time speaking to me. "Damn you're gorgeous! I'm Olivia, what's your name?" She was a lot more friendly than I expected but I welcomed it since I wanted to be quick with our interaction before Chanel noticed. "I'm Moon, and shit I was gonna say the same thing about you! Where you from?" I asked her as I made myself another drink. "I'm originally from California but I have a crib in Orlando and a couple spots in Atlanta and Houston. Where you stay?" She asked me as she finished rolling her blunt. "I'm here from Atlanta myself, we should link next time you there!" I recommended. "Shit that sounds good to me, take my number and shoot me a text so I can lock you in." After exchanging numbers, she took a picture with me for my IG story before we promised to catch up with one another.

I got up and made my way back across the section to where Chanel was seated on some guy's lap. "Girl You ready to get out of here? I'm hungry and tired as fuck." I was ready to call it a night. There were way too many other women there fighting for a piece of the action and too many thirsty ass niggas that were sniffing around for the women unfortunate and desperate enough to fuck with the entourage. Either way I wanted no parts of it and Chanel would never forgive me for letting her hurt and intoxication get in the way of her better judgement.

When we woke up the next morning Chanel had a bad hangover but I knew checkout was in about an hour so I immediately began to pack my bags while she hopped in the shower. I took a break to check my social media and my best friend from back home, Latasha, was facetiming me. "Hey girl! I was just thinking about you." I lied. I really didn't like talking to her because she was always so depressing and she had two kids at this point so she was always distracted and never free to do anything. "Yeah right, then why I haven't heard from you in two weeks? I had to find out on IG that you were in Miami. What's up with that?" She was already giving me the third degree like she was my mother and I was annoyed. "Girl it ain't even like that. This trip was last minute and you know I'm in high demand at the shop since I'm their top stylist, so I just been hella busy. How are you and the boys?"

I'd been quit cosmetology school and used the tuition money my tricks had given me to take trips with Chanel, but as far as everyone back home knew I'd graduated earlier that year and landed a job in one of the hottest celebrity hair salons in Atlanta. I had to figure out a way to keep my family out my business and explain the amount of money at my disposal, so that meant even lying to my best friend. "Um hmm, well me and the boys are cool but shit been crazy up here. You know Trent done left again and left me to have to deal with everything. Keymoney need new shoes he bout to walk out the ones he in." She continued but I zoned her out as I continued to pack and sat the phone down on speaker. I already knew where the conversation was headed so after she was done with her rant, I offered to send her some money. I'd made a lot of money over the weekend so it was nothing to send her $500 to get her off my back. I promised to call her once I made it home and ended the call.

I finished packing before showering and getting dressed, then I was rolling my bags out into the living room of the suite as Chanel stuck her head out of her room and asked me to give her a hand. When I walked in the room the bitch wasn't even halfway packed! She had shit thrown everywhere and was still doing her makeup as she asked, "Can you help me fold some of this shit I know we only got like an hour now right?" Knowing damn well we had 30 minutes before check out. "Girl no we have like half an hour at most and ain't none of your shit packed!" I sucked my teeth and began throwing her shit in bags. "Girl damn you ain't gotta throw my shit like that. You know I have expensive taste, not like yo off the rack shit." I didn't respond I just finished packing up her bags. It took me the full 30 minutes to get her stuff together while she finished getting herself dolled up.

When we got back to Atlanta, I was relieved to go to my apartment without Chanel so that I could get some time to myself. I mean I was cool with the girl but she was super controlling and very jealous. I took the time to call the girl Olivia from the club in Miami and see what she was on. "Hello?" She answered. "Hey Olivia? This is Moon, we met in Miami a couple nights ago. Did I catch you at a bad time?" I poured myself a glass of wine before sitting on my barstool at my island countertop. " Oh, hey beautiful, it's a good time, I'm still laying in the bed right now. You still down here or are you back in Atlanta already?"

"I got back to Atlanta today, I just finished unpacking, enjoying a glass of wine before I order dinner."

"Damn, I was gonna invite you to a private

party tonight. I will be up there in a couple weeks I gotta link up with you when I touch down." She offered. "Yeah, I definitely would've been there too!" I added, happy to welcome some new energy into my life. "What do you do out there in Atlanta?"

"I'm a model." I stated proudly. I hadn't done anything major outside of posting on IG but I had a massive following and was getting paid for ads so I was in fact considered a model. "Interesting." Olivia stated before getting silent. "What is it that you do?" Something about Olivia was alluring and I made it my mission to find out what it was so I was not shy about my questions. Baby girl looked paid and I wanted in! "Well, I do a few things but my main source of income is real estate. I really don't discuss my other businesses over the phone, you single out there or you got you one of them DL ATL niggas?" She asked with a laugh.

It was no secret that a lot of the men in Atlanta played for both teams. A lot of the men were closeted or into certain sex that fed into their homosexual fantasies. Chanel had already told me that they were usually the ones that were willing to pay the most for your silence. "Girl hell nah I'm big single out here in these streets." I responded as I took another swig from my chilled wine.

"Hmmm, how you manage that? You definitely a baddy I can't believe you haven't been wifed up. Oh, shit I gotta take this call, can I call you later?"

CHAPTER FIVE

For the two weeks leading up to her visit to the ATL, Olivia and I spoke daily, texting and small talk mostly but she was pretty cool. I was growing tired of Chanel's superior attitude and King had cut back on the money he was spending and his time with us. Queen had obviously decided to shorten her leash on her husband which meant Chanel was a lot meaner and a lot more controlling. But I felt relieved that a ball player in Chicago had flown her out of town the same weekend that Olivia was coming to Atlanta. I couldn't wait to link with her and the fact that she'd already had us on a list for a private mansion party the night of her arrival made me even more eager to get in good with her so that I could get in on the lifestyle she was living.

I mean I was making good ass money but I was spending it like crazy. My condo was $2,400 per month not including my bills, my hair and makeup for the month would run me about $3,500, I ate out every day so that was another $2,000 to $3,000 a month and to top it off I never wore the same outfit twice so I'd drop up to $6,000 a month on clothes, shoes and jewelry alone. So even with the ballers on my roster I was still breaking even every month.

I had just finished doing my makeup before my doorbell rang. I was dressed in a hot red cocktail dress that was skin tight so I walked slowly to the front door to greet Olivia. When I opened the door, she was ending a phone call and her eyes lit up when she saw me. "Hey girl! Your spot is nice!" She complimented as I welcomed her inside. "Thank you, the living room is right this way I just have to grab my purse and my heels and I'll be ready." I assured her as I made my way towards my bedroom. "Moon, no offense but this dress isn't appropriate for where I'm taking you tonight." I looked down at my revealing dress and was confused. "Come on let me see what you have in your closet." She grabbed my arm and I lead the way.

She had on an all-black cat suit with a drastic cut in-between her breasts that stopped above her belly button and topped it off with a pair of thigh high gold snakeskin boots. "Now don't get me wrong, you working the hell out of this dress but the theme is more of a dominatrix type vibe." I laughed a bit but her face remained straight. "Oh, you serious? Well, I mean I have this all-black leather sleeveless cat suit with the matching chocker that could work." I remembered I'd bought it for a backup Halloween look but never wore it. "Shit put it on and let me see." Olivia insisted, taking a seat in the chair in the corner of my huge closet. She watched attentively as I changed clothes in front of her.

Luckily once I threw on my red leather thigh high boots and switched my jewelry up, I had Olivia's approval. We made our way to the mansion party as I began to film us in the back of the chauffeur driven black SUV while we danced and rapped along with the music. I made Instagram posts the whole ride so I don't really remember where the party was but it was North of Atlanta about 45 minutes outside the city. When we pulled up, we were met at the gate by four security guards that checked the car, our purses and the driver before having us fill out identity cards and placing our cell phones inside of plastic bags. We were then handed NDA's to sign before being allowed into the gate.

"Damn they took my phone I want to post all this shit! This shit nice as fuck!" I exclaimed as we made our way up the winding driveway surrounded by the perfectly manicured yard that had to be over 100 acres. The mansion itself was beautiful! I had never seen a house so big in person. "Ok I know I didn't say anything but this is Lil Saint's Atlanta crib." My eyes got as big as saucers at the mention of my favorite rapper. "Lil Saint? As in *THE* Lil Saint? As in multi-platinum, record breaking, Dolla Records Lil Saint?" I couldn't believe my ears as my heart began to race. "The one and only. Now get yo shit together girl, we almost to the door." Olivia had pulled her mirror out and applied a little more lipstick and gave herself a look over so I did the same. Making sure my red Mac lipstick was popping by adding a thin layer of lip gloss on top. I checked my nose and popped two mints before we felt the car come to a complete stop.

The front door was surrounded by even more security as we were checked again before gaining entry into the home. My heart was racing as I scanned the room with my eyes. A server dressed in a black cocktail dress walked over with a silver serving tray filled with glasses of champagne and handed us both glasses before we made our way past the small crowd of women in the large foyer and into the living room. I noticed a few celebrities but since I signed an NDA, I won't tell you their names but the room was filled with some elite men and women. I noticed Lil Saint out on the patio where there was a stripper pole with two dancers putting on a show as his music blasted through the speakers. The entire scene was unbelievable as I tried to act as nonchalant as possible, diverting my eyes when he caught me looking.

"Let's go over to the pool table." I suggested. "You shoot pool?" Olivia asked as we made our way through the large living room over to where the all-red pool table was. The men standing around were fine as fuck but I had one goal that night and it was Lil Saint. I walked over to one of the guys standing next to the pool stick rack, "Excuse me let me grab one of these." He cocked his head back as if he were shocked that I was really about to shoot some pool. Olivia was smiling as she sipped her champagne. "Fuck it, grab me one too." She added as she sat her glass down on the end of the pool table. "Oh word? Alright now, you my girl and all but ain't no love on this here table now!" I stated as I handed her a stick.

I had been shooting pool since I was 8 years old with my dad and I was really good at it. Before I knew it, I'd gained the attention of the entire room as I did trick shots and beat three contenders. Finally, as I'd hoped, Lil Saint came in to see what all the fuss was about and when he saw my sexy ass standing at his table talking shit and taking names, I had his full attention. "Don't tell me shorty in here whippin y'all niggas ass on this man's table!" He stated, taking his coat off and handing it to one of his homies. "Ah man shawty damn sholl good. She done whipped Nick and Todd ass bad in here. Hell, Shawty whipped her homegirl ass!" The room erupted in laughter as the well-known comedian talked shit. "O, who you done brought up in here girl?" He walked over to Olivia and casually gave her a hug. I couldn't see his eyes because he was wearing a pair of dark black Versace shades but I was sure he hadn't taken his eyes off of me as I remained quiet and knocked the 8 ball in beating my fourth opponent.

I celebrated with a classy twerk before walking over to where Olivia and Lil Saint were standing. "Hey girl I want you to officially meet the man of the hour, Lil Saint. Saint this is my home girl Moon." He gave me a hug and even though he smelled like a pound of weed his dreads had captured the scent of his expensive cologne. "Nice to meet you, I heard you over here talking shit so you must want next on this table?" I asked in a cocky tone. He laughed as his friends said in unison, "Oooooohhhhhhhhhh" Taunting him. "Ok shorty." He stated in his thick New Orleans accent, "Let's see what you got." He rubbed his hands together and walked over to the bar area and retrieved a long black box, retrieving his special pool stick. I couldn't help it as I talked more shit. "Not you got a special stick and still bout to lose." Everyone busted into laughter again and Lil Saint couldn't help but do the same as he walked over and racked up the balls shaking his head, "Shorty I got 5000 in my pocket that I will give you if you beat my ass in my own crib." He was still smiling but I knew he truly thought he stood a chance.

Now I'm sure if he ever tells this story, if I was important enough for him to remember, he will say he let me win. However, that is not the case, I whooped his ass in his own home and he lost the $5,000 bet he put up against me. After everyone calmed down and we all took a shot, Lil Saint asked if he could speak to me in another room. Of course, I said yes and grabbed his hand, letting him lead the way. He took me downstairs into a theater room and sat in one of the huge red chairs in front of the screen, patting his lap for me to join him.

Now normally I would've hopped on his dick right there in that basement but I wanted what Chanel had with King and I wasn't going to get that by letting him hit on the first day he met me. So, I politely walked past him and sat in the seat next to him. "Oh, it's like that?" He asked with a laugh. "You have no idea." I said to him. "Where's my money playa?" I asked, holding my hand out. He laughed hard before going in his pocket and indeed counting out $5000 right there. "Ok now that you paid up your debt we can talk." I smiled with a wink as I placed my winnings inside my Chanel bag.

"You know I let you win but we ain't gotta go into that." We both laughed as he continued, "But I think you're beautiful and I'm trying to see what's up with you." He was crushing hard but I still played it cool even though I was throbbing between my thighs. "I mean I'm interested in seeing what's up with you as well but outside of this element. So why don't you call me and we can make some arrangements to link up for lunch or something." I crossed my legs and looked at him attentively. I felt awkward not having my cell phone but if I wanted a fish this big, I had to gamble.

"Oh, I see, alright slide your number in my phone and be ready to fly out tomorrow with me." He handed me one of his two phones and I gladly placed my number in it before handing it back to him and asking, "What makes you so sure I can just up and leave like that?" He laughed again before standing up and responding, "I'm Lil fucking Saint. Now let's get back upstairs to this wild ass party." He held his hand out for me and helped me up, stealing a kiss in the process. I smiled as he wiped my lipstick off of his lips with the back of his hand and lead me back up the stairs.

The day after the party Lil Saint's manager called me with my flight details for that afternoon. To my surprise when I arrived at the airport in the private car sent for me there was a private jet on the runway waiting for me as the car drove me damn near right up to the door of the plane. When I got inside, I was greeted by the flight attendant who asked what I was drinking. I ordered a screw driver to keep it simple as I walked down the aisle where Lil Saint was speaking to his manager and looking at a laptop.

There were two other women on the plane but I didn't give a fuck. I was dead set on hooking him no matter what. "Hey everyone." I stated as I entered. They all greeted me and I took one of the open seats closest to where Lil Saint was. I'd never been on a private jet but I damn sure wasn't going to let on that I hadn't. Olivia had already given me a crash course on how to deal with him so I was ready for this trip with him even though I had no idea the destination.

After the two other females and I got acquainted Lil Saint finally ended his conversation with his manager and came over to where I was seated and took the seat in front of me which was also facing me. "Damn you showed up looking good enough to eat." He complimented me as he stared at my cleavage in my red halter top. I peeped red was his favorite color from everything in his house and the fact that the gang he always claimed was in fact the bloods. "Why thank you, I was going for the snack look." I responded with a laugh. Olivia had let me know he loved down to earth funny girls who weren't afraid to let their hair down and get dirty every now and then. So, since that wasn't far from my natural personality, I didn't really have to try hard to be someone I was not.

We talked and laughed the entire flight and when we landed, I couldn't believe my eyes when I realized this man had flown me to muthafuckin St. Barts! I'd never been out of the country let alone to a Caribbean island so I made it up right there on the walk from the jet to the SUV that I was fucking him as soon as he tried again. Fuck that! In my mind I'm like this nigga dropped a real bag to bring me to an island how many hoes could say that? 25 minutes after leaving the private airport we were pulling up to the villa we'd all be staying in for the week.

I was in paradise, literally, as we entered the main suite of the villa. To my surprise the two other girls from the plane placed their bags on the bed right along with me. Just as quickly as I'd thought I was special I found out he'd flown those two bitches out there to do the same shit he was trying to do with me. I could hear Olivia's voice in the back of my mind urging me to stand my ground with him. I turned and walked into the bathroom where he was looking at himself in the mirror and folded my arms. "What's wrong with you?" He asked, turning to face me. "I don't do other bitches, if having you means sharing with some random basic hoes, I'll call a cab and head right back to the airport."

I really was hoping that man didn't tell me to go fuck myself and show me to the front door but I had to play the game. He smirked before walking past me, smacking me on the ass and telling the girls they'd be staying in one of the other guest rooms. I smiled at myself in the mirror as I watched him walk them out of the master suite. I took that time to hop in the shower and get changed into something sexy. Chanel and I had gotten a lot of new lingerie the previous weekend so I picked out a red lacy number and laid it across the bed, then grabbed my smaller bag that held all my toiletries inside before throwing my hair into a shower cap and stepping into the shower.

While I was bathing myself, I heard the shower door slide open and Lil Saint was standing there with his shirt off and a fat blunt in his mouth. "So, if you made me get rid of them chicks that must mean you think you enough for me?" He asked as he inhaled the marijuana smoke deeply. I felt like I was in a music video standing this close to Lil Saint while I was butt ass naked. I don't know whose personality took over me out of Olivia and Chanel but either way I said fuck it and went after what I wanted. "I'm more than enough,

I'm gonna be your good little girl, now tell me what daddy needs after that long ass flight?" I was using my most feminine low tone as I spoke seductively.

He went to take off his belt and I stopped him, doing it for him, before his pants fell down to his ankle. He stepped out of them and then stepped out of his boxers before joining me in the shower. His dick wasn't as big as I'd expected, which was a little disappointing, but the way I moaned for him you would've thought he was the best I'd ever had. We fucked for all of 12 minutes before he was cumming hard onto my ass.

After the week-long St. Barts trip, I was locked in with Lil Saint. We'd been dating for a little over three months and he'd taken me to 9 of the 50 states and added Europe to my passport. Although he was one of the wealthiest black men in the game he was extremely controlling with his money. He'd forbidden me from dating other men but he would literally have me send him my bills for him to pay and when I wanted to go shopping, even for groceries, he would only send me money once I was at the register and facetimed him to show him the total. I wasn't getting an allowance but he was definitely spoiling me.

I was walking out of the spa when my mother was calling my phone for the third time in an hour. I didn't feel like talking to her but I answered the phone. She was talking so fast I could barely understand her before attempting to calm her down. "Ma slow down I can't understand you." She fell silent as she attempted to pace her breathing but she was still hysterical as my father got on the phone. "Moon, you need to get on the next flight up here. Your brother is in the hospital." His voice was calm but shaky and I could tell he'd been crying. "Daddy is it MJ?" I panicked as I grabbed at my chest. "Yes Princess, how soon can you get here? It doesn't look good."

I was heartbroken as I assured my father that I'd get the flight info and get to St. Louis before the sun went down. I immediately called Lil Saint who answered on the fourth ring. "What up?" He asked, background filled with commotion. "I'm at the studio so talk fast lil momma."

"Baby my big brother is in the hospital, my parents just called me and said I need to get there it doesn't look good." I burst into tears as the seriousness of the situation hit me. I couldn't believe MJ was in the hospital. He'd been doing his own clothing line heavy back home and had created a buzz for himself since graduating from college a couple years prior. I'd missed his graduation because I was in LA with Chanel fucking with some athletes, who shall remain nameless.

I was regretting it in this moment as so many scenarios went through my head about what could've happened to my big brother. Lil Saint didn't hesitate he, shockingly, cut me off and said, "Say less, book the flight I'm about to transfer you some money now. Let me know if you need anything, I'll be here."

"Thank you so much baby I am so scared." I admitted through sobs. "I know but try to calm down and handle your business so you can get to your family. The money in your account call me when your flight land, do you need me to get you a car to grab you from the airport?" He offered. I couldn't believe how nice and generous he was being because he was normally kind of mean. Not really in a disrespectful way but in a "I'm God, bow down to me." type of way. He had transferred $5,000 into my account and that was the most money he'd ever given me without seeing a receipt first. "Yes please, I'll get you the info once it's booked. I'm headed to the house now to pack a bag."

The next available flight had me in St. Louis four hours later and as a black SUV dropped me off at the front of the hospital as I was looking down at my phone to make sure I had the room information my dad had text me. With my Gucci travel bag thrown over my shoulder I made my way towards the ICU and saw my other brother Marvin pacing in the waiting room. "Marv!?" I called out before running towards him as he opened his arms. As we embraced, he let out everything he'd obviously been holding in. Marvin and I were literally 10 months apart. He and I were the closest out of all my brothers and him breaking down had put me in a panic. "What is going on Marv? Y'all scaring me, what happened to MJ?" I was so scared to hear what he had to say but I had to know. "They shot him Moon! Them fuck ass pigs shot him!" My mouth fell open at his revelation.

"THE COPS?!" I yelled angrily. "The fucking cops Moon! The fucking cops shot him!" I'd never seen my brother this emotional. "Where is he? I have to see him!" I held his hand as we walked through the set of double doors that led into the ICU. Just as my other brother Marshawn was coming out. We embraced silently for just a moment as they walked me to MJ's room. I could not believe my brother was in a hospital bed with 8 bullet holes in his body at the hands of the police.

The city hadn't been the same since Mike Brown had been murdered two years prior. If you don't remember Mike Brown, he was the 18 years young black man who was gunned down by 28-year-old Ferguson police officer Darren Wilson, which is public information. The city had been at war ever since even with some of the activists being murdered and Mike's memorial being set on fire. I still remember when everything first went down and me thinking about my brothers and how it could've easily been them as the next hashtag and how far I was away from them since I'd just moved to Atlanta right before it happened. But now, in that moment, I couldn't help but wonder if MJ would end up being just that.

My parents were shocked to see me as they both came from inside the room and grabbed me close. "Daddy what happened?" I asked as they finally released me. My mother, Meshaun, was so distraught she couldn't even say any words as she returned to MJ's bed side. "Y'all go in there and stay with your mother while I talk to your sister." My father instructed my older brothers who silently complied.

"Moon your brothers were on the way back to their apartment last night and were pulled over by the police. They said they smelled weed but you know you and your brothers don't do any drugs! I didn't raise y'all like that. They had MJ and Marshawn outside the car and Marshawn said the cop was being extra rough on him for no reason and all of a sudden he just heard the cop begin yelling at MJ before he heard a whole bunch of shots." My dad rubbed his eyes to ensure no tears actually fell but I could tell he was heartbroken and very worried about MJ's fate. "Oh my God! Why would they shoot him? MJ wouldn't hurt a fly." I just couldn't wrap my head around it.

I didn't want to stay the night at the hospital and I damn sure didn't want to stay at my parent's small ass apartment so two hours after I arrived, I kissed my family good night and promised to return the next morning. I waited for the private car to pull back up and I headed downtown to the Hotel St. Louis. When I checked into the hotel, I finally called Latasha back. She'd been blowing up my phone the entire day. I knew it was about MJ but I didn't really feel like talking about it. "Hey girl." I answered the phone trying to sound extra sad. "Moon I heard about MJ! Are you okay? Do you guys need anything?"

The crazy thing is, I knew that Latasha had my back and loved me like a sister, but the person I was in Atlanta wasn't the person she knew anymore and I guess a part of me tried my best to blame her for my shame of my double life by pushing her away. "Yeah, we good, we don't need anything." I stated with a little attitude. "Moon, you ok? Are you coming back home?" Latasha didn't care that I was being dry with her. I did miss our genuine connection but I had to lie so much every time we spoke it was exhausting.

"I got here earlier today I been at the hospital with the fam." I was lying across the bed smoking my vape pen as I spoke. "What? Where are you staying? My mom actually kept the kids today so I can pull up if you want!" I figured I might as well get the interaction out the way and as long as she didn't have them crying ass bad ass babies, I was cool with seeing her. "I'm downtown at the St. Louis. Stop and grab a bottle a bitch need a drink, I'll CashApp you." I already knew she was gonna say she didn't have the money for the shit I drank so I sent the money and got off the bed to shower and change into my pajamas. "I want Henny, the big bottle and grab some cranberry juice for us." After hanging up the phone I text her my room number and got inside the running shower.

When Latasha arrived, she was so excited to see me. I tried my best to fake the emotion and I guess it worked. I hugged her hard and looked her up and down. She'd gained at least 60 pounds since the last time I'd seen her and I couldn't help but think that was why she didn't really post on social media anymore unless it was posts of her sons. "Oh, my goodness girl you looking good as fuck! I love your hair. I can't believe you are here!" She was so excited as she looked around my suite. "This room is lit as fuck Moon! You done went to Atlanta and blew the fuck up!" She yelled loudly as she plopped down on the couch. "Bitch I need to come to Atlanta with you and get my glow up on too. Between the boys and they daddies I am being ran ragged." I took a seat on the couch next to her and turned the tv on. "Girl let's get this bottle open before you get all deep on me. It sounds like you need one as well."

I walked into the kitchen of the suite and grabbed a couple of glasses before she continued. "Girl I know I need a damn drink. Shit been crazy up here. Then you know me and Tracy been beefing, we got into a fight at the spot like two months ago." I rolled my eyes as I began making our drinks, being sure to be generous with the Hennessey in both of our cups. I was over the drama between her baby father's other baby mother already as I drained out her rant. I handed her a cup as she continued and downed half my cup as I acted as if I were interested in her conversation.

After 25 minutes of her going on and on about her depressing ass existence I was tipsy. I grabbed the bottle to start on my second drink before Latasha finally stopped to take a sip from her own. "Damn I must just be running my mouth! You already on your second cup I gotta catch up." She said with a laugh. "Yeah, I needed this." I added, my best attempt at sounding sad, in actuality I just wanted to get lit. "My bad boo, I've just been talking all about me, how is MJ?"

"He's holding on, the fucking cops shot him so many times it's scary." I took a shot from the bottle before sitting it back on the table. My phone rang and I had to excuse myself as I ran to the bedroom and answered my facetime. "Hey baby! I just checked into the hotel not too long ago I was just about to call you." It was Lil Saint and he was surrounded by bitches in his LA house. I ignored it because I knew he fucked with other women. "How is your brother?" He asked as he puffed from his blunt. "He's ok, they have him on 24-hour watch and my parents are staying at the hospital with them." I sat on the end of the bed as I smiled from ear to ear as I stared at him in the phone. "I'm glad he good cause I need you to come out to Barcelona with me. Your flight will bring you here the day after tomorrow and we'll fly out together. I gotta dip now but Leon will send you over the itinerary. Call me tomorrow."

When I walked back out into the living room Latasha was still seated on the couch. "Let's take some shots!" I exclaimed, excited from the news of the new stamp I'd get on my passport.

CHAPTER SIX

"Your brother laying in there clinging on for dear life and you just finna leave?" I could tell my father was angry because he never raised his voice at me but as we stood in the hospital waiting room, he let me have it as my other brothers watched from the side of him. "Dad I have to go, it's business. I will be back in like a week tops." I didn't care what my dad or mom said I was getting on that flight to LA so I could head to Barcelona with my man. "I can't believe you right now! You done went down there to Atlanta and lost yo damn mind." I knew my dad was very disappointed in me, and the girl I was 3 years prior would've broken down at the thought of it, but the woman I was becoming didn't want to sit there all sad and shit when I had the option to be in fucking BARCELONA!

"Dad I'm sorry but I really gotta go, I'll call y'all when I land." I reached out to give my dad a hug and he backed away from me, shaking his head, "Don't bother." Was the only thing he said as he dropped his shoulders and walked back through the double doors defeated. I really tried my hardest to put on a sad face for my brothers but inside I truly didn't give a fuck. I was ready to get on that plane and get to my fine ass; rich ass man.

"What? Y'all bout to lecture me to?" I asked my brothers who were standing there in silence. "Nah sis, be safe. Let me know when you land." Marvin assured me with a one-armed hug. "Yeah, we'll keep you posted with MJ." Marshawn added as he wrapped his arm around my neck to give me a big hug. "I love y'all." I told them as I picked up my bag out of one of the chairs and pushed my designer shades back onto my face before walking outside to meet the private car that had been waiting on me.

When we got to Barcelona we were staying at the Mandarin Oriental. If you've never heard of it please look it up because it was absolutely beautiful! Of course, we weren't alone on the trip, there was about 16 of us total staying at the hotel. After we got to the room, I made my way into the bedroom to shower and change. I put on a red PVC Mini dress that hugged my body just right. Saint walked in the bathroom, smacking my ass and saying, "Damn you looking good as hell baby." His New Orleans accent always drove me wild especially how he said the word *baby*. "Thank you daddy. What's on the agenda for tonight?" I asked as I did my makeup.

"Everybody bout to come through so we can figure it out. But before you finish doing your makeup and shit why don't you come show daddy some love." He grabbed at his dick through his Fendi jogging pants. "I got you." I smiled as I literally dropped everything in my hands and got down on my knees in front of him and pleased him, swallowing his kids and all.

I brushed my teeth and gargled mouthwash as Saint started the shower. "You put my clothes out?" He asked me as he made his way back out into the room. "Yeah, your clothes are hanging in the closet." I responded as I continued putting my makeup on.

After I finished making myself up, I heard someone at the door and since Saint was still in the shower, I went to open it. It was a crew of people coming to set up the catered food ordered for the night. While they were setting up, some of Saint's crew began to arrive and I got the bar set up so that we could start popping some bottles. I was always pretty quiet when his friends and groupies were around, mostly because Saint didn't like friendly chicks. A lot of girls play themselves out of real ballers by being too friendly to their crew. They aren't into it and their egos won't allow them to fall for a chick they feel will talk to the next highest bidder.

The party in the suite was in full affect as blunts were rolled, liquor was poured, music blasting and the vibes were high. I watched as a few of his crew members entered the suite with 6 random women they'd found somewhere in the hotel or on the streets, who knows. But the females began mingling and drinking immediately. They were very loud and obnoxious so I continued getting drunk as fuck while I watched from the bar. Saint had come over to me and I could tell he was feeling good. "Come here babe." He said to me, grabbing me around my waist and pulling me back towards him.

He walked me into our suite and there was a chick in black lingerie lying across our bed. My initial reaction was disappointment because I honestly wasn't into women. What Chanel and I had was different because I looked at it as a business deal. Saint had money like King but he was nowhere near as generous so adding bitches to the equation was not in the cards for me. "Baby, what is going on? You know I'm not into chicks." I tried to be as sweet as I could as I spoke. "I know but she's here as a gift to you. You ain't gotta do shit, she gonna please you." He pulled me close and began kissing me. I mean the chick was very attractive and had a banging ass body and again this was Lil Saint! While he was kissing me, he picked me up and walked me over to the bed, dropping me down on the bed and taking his Shirt off.

The girl seated on the bed began to run her fingers through my hair as Saint continued to kiss and lick on my lips and neck. I allowed the liquor in me to take over as I leaned back on the bed and allowed her to pull my dress up and begin licking on my pussy through my panties, which were already soaked from my juices. She moved my panties to the side and inserted a finger while Saint started to remove his pants. "Just enjoy it baby girl, let me taste you." The girl said to me as I lifted my hips to allow her to remove my panties. I relaxed and allowed myself to enjoy the pleasure she was giving me as she swirled her tongue over my clit. I watched Saint put a condom on before entering her from behind. She moaned as she continued to orally please me and I was loving it.

We fucked in every position you can imagine and that was the first night I actually saw Saint do coke with my own eyes. I'd heard rumors that he was into some crazy drugs but the few months we'd been dating I'd only ever seen him smoke weed and drink lean every now and then. But I didn't give a fuck, I looked at is as he trusted me enough to not hide it from me anymore. Which, to me, meant he was starting to fall for me. The girl and I took a shower while Saint watched as he rolled up another blunt. We lathered up soap on one another and were kissing on each other for Saint's enjoyment. He had a big smile on his face as he finished pearling his backwoods, placing it on the counter, and stepping in the shower to join us.

We never made it back to the party that night but we spent the rest of the trip with the girl, whose name I didn't find out until the next day when we all went to the Palace of Catalan Music; one of the top tourists attractions in Barcelona. The girl, Naomi, turned out to be pretty cool and was from the states as well. She lived in Dallas, Texas, and was a few months older than I was. Since my 21st birthday was approaching I'd made it a point to exchange our information and promised to invite her to the festivities.

I had been taking pictures the entire trip but Saint was very strict on my posting so I couldn't wait to get home to stunt on bitches. When my flight arrived back in Atlanta, I finally decided to take my phone off of do not disturb mode and was immediately notified of hundreds of texts and voicemails. I began listening to the voicemails from the backseat of the private car escorting me home.

Come to find out MJ did not survive his injuries and had passed away two days after I'd left St. Louis. He was dead at 23 years old and I felt like I couldn't breathe as I finally got my brother Marvin on the phone. "Marv tell me this shit ain't true!" I sobbed as I began to break down. I could hear a lot of different voices in his background before I heard my father's voice in the receiver. "Princess Marie Simmons, I can forgive and forget a lot of things but you leaving your family in a time of need and missing your own brother's funeral isn't one of them. I really hope you enjoyed the last week. I pray that it was worth it for you. You have broken our hearts and I honestly don't see how you could possibly fix this. Now Marvin and I have to go, we have to go watch your brother get lowered into the ground."

I couldn't believe I'd fucked up so bad, I could hear and feel the hurt in my father's voice but honestly, I didn't regret going to Barcelona! At that time, I was so far away from being daddy's little girl that I almost took his words as a challenge. He wanted to cut me off? Well, I was going to show him I didn't need shit from them anyway.

CHAPTER SEVEN

"Bitch look at this!" Chanel exclaimed as I walked into her crib with a bottle of champagne to celebrate her house warming. She'd finally gotten her own real crib, from King, and I was happy for her and jealous of her at the same damn time. She definitely knew how to milk a nigga and seeing her huge crib in Buckhead with the 80-foot ceilings, home theater and wine cellar. Not to mention the enclosed pool and jacuzzi area which had a sauna room built in; was inspiring to say the least. She was so hype as she gave me a tour of her crib.

At this point I'd been dating Lil Saint for five months and I was beginning to grow tired of all the random women he'd been bringing to join us in the bedroom. He still hadn't become as generous as King but he was doing better with adding a $5,000 a month allowance on top of my bills he was paying, but seeing how Chanel was getting it, I wanted more. I hadn't heard from my parents in the two months after MJ's death and although Marvin would text me every now and then I could tell I'd broken his heart as well.

"Damn this nigga really went all out didn't he?" I was admiring the huge chandelier in her dining room above her Versace dining table. "Girl this was a parting gift. He better had gone all the way out!" She went on to explain how since Queen was now pregnant with King's twins, he'd decided to actually give his marriage a fair shot. The fact that Queen publicly put out a project that alluded to King cheating was most likely the driving factor; either way Chanel got a $800,000 crib and a $1.5M check out of it and she was happy with that. I hadn't talked to King in months at this point so he was just an exciting memory as far as I was concerned.

She walked me out onto the patio that overlooked her huge backyard and continued, "Moon I put in a lot of time with King and I was loyal, I mean a bitch knew it wouldn't last forever but I thought I was at least worth a final face to face. You know this nigga had his lawyer come to my spot and bring me the paperwork and the deed? He didn't even give me the courtesy of a good bye fuck." She laughed but I could tell she was hurt.

Chanel had trained herself to show no emotions but her tough exterior was cracking. I walked over to her and gave her a hug. "Girl you know how these niggas are. He gone be right back on yo line begging for you to come back, watch. A nigga ain't just dropping this type of shit on hoes he don't fuck with. Now chill with the sentimental shit and take a look around! You did it bitch! This nigga bought you a muthafuckin house house!" We both burst into laughter before Chanel added, "Girl you right though, now pop that bottle so we can turn up before these people start pulling up." I didn't hesitate before shaking the champagne up a bit and popping it open, as it bubbled up and erupted from the opening. "Ayyyyyyyyeeee!" We screamed before drinking it straight from the bottle.

Chanel had planned a small get together of friends and family to help celebrate her new home. There was about 15 people in attendance but the only ones I was focused on were the three ball players that had joined Chanel's new boo, and were walking through the door as we were all watching a few people play Jenga. "Oh, bitch that's ole boy that play for Chicago." Chanel said with a wink as she grabbed my arm and lead me in their direction with her. "They fine as fuck!" I whispered as we approached them. "Hey baby, I'm glad you could make it." She greeted him with a hug as he leaned down and kissed her on the forehead. "No doubt, I hope you don't mind I brought a few of my guys with me. Chanel this is Titus, Lance and D guys this is the lady of the hour, Chanel."

They all greeted her and complimented her home before she introduced me to them. I was very attracted to Titus but either of them could've got it. "Well make yourselves at home, the food is in the dining area over to the left of the stairs and the bar is downstairs. There's also a pool table and game system in the theater if y'all are interested."

"Well shit which way to the food cause a nigga hungry no cap!" The guy her friend introduced as D asked. "Come on just follow me, babe you hungry too?" She asked her boo as they all followed her towards the dining room.

Titus must've felt the energy I was throwing his direction because he stayed behind and asked me to show him to the bar. You know I was cheesing like a damn fool as I grabbed his hand and walked him down in the basement area. "This crib almost as big as my shit, ya girl doing her thing out here in the ATL." He said as we walked past a few other guests as they enjoyed a game of pool. "Yeah, she definitely winning right now, what you like to drink?" I asked him as we made it to the bar. "I'm a dark and straight type nigga, what she got back there? Look like a fully stocked joint." He took a seat on one of the bar stools as I walked behind the bar to make him a drink.

"So, you play for Chicago too?" I asked as I poured both of us shots of Hennessey. He laughed before answering, "Nah I play for the Lakers ma. I take it you don't watch basketball?" I knew exactly who he was but it was all a part of my game. "I mean I watch it sometimes but not enough to know who's who." I handed him his shot and we took them together before I began to pour another round. "Yeah, I live out in Cali but we here for the weekend. You trying to kick it with me for the weekend?" He asked before we downed the second shot. "I mean I guess we could make that happen." I smiled shyly. "I can't lie, you a bad mufukka. I know niggas probably all on yo line."

"It's not even like that." I stated as I made myself a cocktail and poured him a glass of Hen on ice. "Then what's it like? Cause ain't no way nobody getting at all of that." He grinned. "I just be chilling for real. I talk to a person I'm feeling but I don't belong to anybody." I was really feeling this nigga. He was so damn sexy and the way he never took his eyes off of mine did something to me. "Well then you coming with me tonight?" He asked boldly. I was horny as fuck and I knew if I went with him, we would definitely fuck that night so I attempted to decline. "Tonight? I just met you I don't even know you." I made a confused face as I laughed. "It ain't even like that ma, I'm not trying to make you do anything you don't wanna do. I ain't no thirsty ass nigga. I just like what I see and wanna see if the mind match that's all."

Needless to say, we ditched the party and I took my fast ass right to the Air BNB that he'd rented for the weekend. When we arrived, he had me pull into the garage before I could get out of the car. We walked inside and he didn't waste any time trying to get in-between my legs. Scooping me up and sitting me on the table in the kitchen, lifting up my dress and shoving his head between my legs. The head was sloppy as fuck but I moaned as I tried my best to guide him in the right direction. He finished after a good five or six minutes and then came up to kiss me before picking me back up, wrapping my legs around his waist, and taking my in the living room. "Slow down big boy. I'm not trying to fuck." I pulled my dress back down and looked up at him. "Shit, is it money? Cause I know niggas paying for that wet ass pussy." He grabbed his dick and pulled it out of his pants to show off his 10 inches. "I got like seven K on me right now, what's up?"

After he gave me the money I got up off the couch and had him sit down to get comfortable. I got on my knees in front of him and began massaging his erect penis with the back of my throat. He was moaning as I caressed his balls with my fingers and began scooting forward, pushing my head down towards his ass. I was not into the whole ass eating thing but I began licking his gooch and it didn't take another minute for him to explode into my hand. "God damn girl!" He exclaimed as he paced his breathing. I got up off the floor and asked him where the bathroom was.

He walked me upstairs to the master bedroom and I went inside the bathroom and closed the door behind me. I quickly grabbed his toothpaste and a clean washcloth and scrubbed my tongue with both before rinsing my mouth with mouthwash. I took my dress off and hung it on the back of the bathroom door before returning to the bedroom where Titus was laying back on the bed fully undressed massaging his penis. "Oh, you ready for me huh?" I teased him, slowly walking towards him as I unsnapped my bra and took it off seductively. He was biting on his bottom lip as I approached him and allowed my bra to hit the floor exposing my perfect perky breasts. "Shit! Come sit on daddy dick."

"Where's your rubber?" I asked him as I got on the bed. "I'm clean baby, come here." He said, sitting up and sucking on my breasts as I straddled him. I can't lie, and I know it wasn't smart, I was horny as fuck as he rubbed his dick against my clit through my laced panties while he sucked on my neck and breasts. I began grinding back as he continued to lick on me while pulling my panties to the side and sliding inside of me. That shit felt so good as I moaned and began winding my hips and practicing my keegles with his dick. I pushed him to lie back as sat up briefly to take my panties off. I was dripping wet as I propped both my feet up on the bed in the squatting position and lowered myself back onto him. "Ohh, hell yeah." He exclaimed as I began winding on him spelling out COCONUT with my hips, something Chanel had taught me.

He couldn't take my riding skills for too long because buddy was begging me to get up after only a few minutes and got back down and started eating me out. I was rubbing my hand on the back of his head as I rubbed my breast with my other one. He was going crazy as I exploded, squirting, all over his face. He flipped me over and grabbed both of my arms from behind before he eased all of himself inside me. He pulled back on my arms as he picked up the pace and that shit was LIFE! He let go of my arms and began smacking my ass hard before pulling out and nutting on it.

"Oh yeah, I can already tell you gonna be trouble." I turned back over on the bed and fixed my hair before responding, "Good trouble or bad trouble?" I smiled at him as he looked in my eyes. "Shit probably both of em. But with that pussy you sitting on I can almost guarantee it's worth me finding out, now come sit that pretty mufukka on my face."

Titus was pretty cool and after the first two months of us fucking around our hot romance slowed down. We would link anytime he came to Atlanta but with me and Saint flying all over the world I wasn't always available. I mean honestly, he was a typical athlete, very flashy and loose with his money but I was fine with that because it wasn't like I was trying to marry the nigga. As long as he continued to ice my wrist and contribute to my bank account I was satisfied, the good dick was only a bonus. I figured if Lil Saint wasn't going to get me into a crib like Chanel's then there was no way I was going to keep all my eggs in one basket. I enjoyed my time with him and even though we'd cooled off we were still speaking pretty regularly.

CHAPTER EIGHT

My 21st birthday rolled around pretty quickly and I was pleasantly surprised that Saint had decided to bare no expense when it came to my party. Titus had even given me $10,000 as a birthday gift but he couldn't make it to the party. Olivia had been helping me with her connects in Atlanta to make my vision come together and with me turning 21 it had to be special. I decided on a Moulin Rouge themed party and I knew it was about to be lit! Saint rented out a mansion for me and had my favorite restaurant, Imperial Fez, cater the night. The house was equipped with three fully stocked bars, and I'd hired an authentic Burlesque group, aerial silk dancers and even fire dancers to put on shows throughout the night.

In true Moulin Rouge fashion, I had to have a red carpet and a huge red and black corset shaped cake. The red Gucci dress I was rocking for the night had been made custom to fit me perfectly. The way the red feathers poked out made me resemble a cute peacock and the dramatic fascinator on my head was sure to remind everyone in attendance just who the lady of the hour was. I was seated in one of the upstairs bathrooms getting my hair and makeup done by the glam squad I'd hired for the day when Olivia arrived, bottle in hand, "Happy birthday girl!" She screamed as she entered, giving me a hug and complimenting my hair, which was pinned up at the top and flowing with big curls at the bottom.

"Girl thank you! I don't know why I'm nervous!" I admitted as Olivia began digging in her purse looking for something. "Could this be why?" She asked, pulling out her phone and showing me pictures of Saint and I in Miami the weekend prior leaving the Hyde hotel. "Bitch, how they just now getting these pictures on your birthday?" She asked as I pulled out my phone to check my Instagram. Just like that my following had tripled from my name being tied to Saint. My eyes lit up as I began smiling. "Girl he must not have seen this cause he ain't mention it when I just talked to him." I was swiping through all of the blogs IG pages to see the posts about me.

"He don't care about that IG shit and he gets tied to new bitches every other day. Don't sweat it, but where yo cup at? It's a celebration ain't it?" Olivia stated as she opened the bottle of Dusse' she'd brought. I didn't care how many women he'd been tied to, the fact that I was on the blogs and people were discussing me was a natural high all on its own.

Since I'd met Olivia seven months prior, we'd gotten really close, well as close as we could with her being so protective of her personal life. She and I would talk daily and link up every chance we could. Olivia was a real boss chick who was about her paper and she had so much respect amongst every circle I'd seen her in but I'd never seen her in blogs or even with a man that she was dating.

"Well, I'm about to go down the hall and get dressed, the DJ is in route and the valet company just arrived and are setting up. They have the stage complete and the dancers are doing their final run through right now. So, take this bottle, relax and enjoy your night!" She handed me the bottle and gave me a kiss on the cheek. "Thank you, girl I really appreciate, you." I responded before she headed back out of the bathroom. Just then my phone rang and it was Latasha. I ignored her call for the fifth time that day but when she called right back, I went ahead and answered for her. "Yeah? What's up?" I answered in a hurried tone. "Damn I been trying to reach you since this morning! Bitch you dating Lil Saint and you ain't tell me? I would be cursing you out if it wasn't your birthday!" She sounded so excited as she spoke. "But happy birthday Moon! What you doing today?"

"Thank you Tasha, and my homegirl throwing me a party. I'm getting my hair and makeup done now, can I call you back later?"

"Yo homegirl, who, Chanel? Oh, see hell nah I need to know the tea with you and Lil Saint bitch!"

"Girl I will fill you in tomorrow I promise, it's too much going on right now but I got you. I love you girl but I gotta catch up with you tomorrow ok?" I was in no mood discussing my business in front of the makeup artist and hair stylist. "Um hmm, you better call me too or I'm gone be blowing yo phone up cause this some big news!" I could tell she was hesitant on taking my word since I had been so bad at being there for her since I'd moved to Atlanta but I couldn't have cared less. I ended the call and took a shot from the Dusse' bottle before the MUA painted on my lipstick.

The party was in full effect when someone walked up behind me as I watched the Burlesque show, tapping my shoulder, yelling "Happy birthday mama!" I screamed in excitement when I recognized Naomi, the chick I'd met in Barcelona, "You made it! I thought you said you missed your flight!" I embraced her with a friendly hug. "I wanted to surprise you! There was no way I was missing this, girl this shit lit, you got a lot of damn friends!" She complimented as she looked around the room.

"Girl I don't even know half of these people and majority of them only here in hopes of seeing Saint." I confessed with a laugh. "Is he even pulling up?" She asked me as she took a sip from the drink in her hand. "Nah he had some business to attend to out Vegas but I'm flying out there tomorrow to kick it with him, ooohh you should come out there with me!" I liked Naomi's vibe and at least I somewhat knew her. I didn't want to be licking on random cooch on my birthday weekend, even though at this point I'd been with so many women I'd lost count. "Well don't look like I have a choice bitch I flew out here to kick it with yo ass for the weekend!" She as she laughed. "Well then it's settled I'll book your flight right now! We gone have so much fun."

Chanel finally decided to grace us with her presence, arriving four hours late and accompanied by a group of her homegirls, the same ones I'd met her with three years prior. "Damn girl I thought it'd be more ballers here! Guess Saint got you on yo good girl routine." She said with a smirk as her friends all shared a laugh at a joke I'd obviously missed.

"Girl it's so many people here you just walked in the door, let me show y'all around, this is my girl Naomi from Texas. Naomi this is my girl Chanel and these are her close friends. We were all about to head outside for the second show! Let's get some glasses in y'all hands so we can make a toast!" I could feel the tension but I didn't know where it was coming from so I attempted to lighten the mood.

We all walked outside into the back yard where I had a huge ice sculpture in the shape of the number 21 that was behind the outside bar. We vibed to the music the DJ was mixing as several people came up to me to take pictures and give me birthday wishes. "Damn you went all the way out girl! This shit nice as fuck!" Naomi complimented as she admired the set up outside. Chanel and her friends were kind of falling behind as they whispered and laughed with one another. I'm guessing Naomi felt the vibe because she excused herself to the bathroom and left me standing there with them. "So, I guess you and that nigga must be official since he going all out for your birthday and shit huh?" Chanel asked with a slick grin.

"I mean we just enjoying each other right now that's all." I informed her as I ordered a round of drinks for the group. "Ummm hmmm, y'all look pretty official on the blogs today." She added. "Well, you know we can't control what these blogs post. Those pictures are like a week or so old I don't know how the blogs got them anyway. But here's your shots ladies, the fire dancers will be starting the show soon. Let me go make sure everything is good, I'll be back."

I wasn't really sure why Chanel's energy seemed off but I wasn't going to allow her to ruin my night. Ever since King cut her off, she'd been in a nasty ass mood and there was no way I was going to be a part of her wrath on my birthday. I walked around the party ensuring that my guests were enjoying themselves and I made sure I posted it all on my IG story. The fire dancers had begun their show and the crowd went crazy! I stood on the balcony looking down at the crowd as I just took it all in. I couldn't believe my luck at just 21 years old I felt established and free.

As I watched and sipped my champagne someone walked up behind me and began kissing the back of my neck. I spun around and it was Chanel, grinning as she stuck her hand up my dress. "Chanel girl stttopp." I moaned a bit as she began licking on my neck, putting her fingers inside of me. I began grinding against them as she started to kiss me. I can't lie no matter what Chanel did or how she treated me that bitch could turn me on like no other. She pulled me inside and closed the door to the patio of the room we were in before pulling me over to the bed. "Let me taste you." She said, pushing the fingers she'd just taken out of me inside her mouth. I pulled my panties down before lying back on the bed.

Chanel joined me and straddled my waste before reaching down in-between her breasts and pulling out a pill and placing it in her mouth. She leaned down and tongue kissed me while pushing the pill down my throat with her tongue. I was feeling good as fuck and Chanel and I had done Molly, X and coke together so I didn't think twice before swallowing the pill as she disappeared between my legs. I felt her soft warm tongue trailing up my thigh as I rubbed my hands through her hair letting out soft moans of ecstasy. She swirled her tongue, softly sucking my thighs, before coming up to tease me.

Flicking her tongue over my hardening clit, she began to finger me again, instantly finding my G-spot. "Oh shit, right there, I'm about to cum." I blurted out before I began squirting into her mouth. But she didn't stop. She began eating my pussy so good I felt waves going through my body. The next thing I knew someone was walking into the room but I was so drunk and high I didn't care as I pushed her face into my wet throbbing opening.

Now what happened next, I'm not too sure of because I didn't find out until later that Chanel hadn't given me Molly or X, she'd given me Rohypnol, known on the street as "Roofies" or the date rape drug. But we'll get back to that later.

The next morning, I awakened on the bed in the guest bedroom of the rented house. Surprisingly I didn't have a headache or feel hungover but for the life of me I couldn't remember anything past Chanel and I having sex. I searched for my phone and found it under one of the pillows. I had several missed calls from Olivia and Naomi so I called Olivia first to see if she could fill me in on the events from the night. "Hey girl, you good?" She answered on the first ring. "Yeah, I have no idea what happened last night. Like I literally am drawing a blank." I expressed as I slid out of the bed and walked out of the room.

The cleaning crew had already arrived as I made my way into the master bedroom to begin getting myself together. "Girl all I know is you were knocked out cold when I came looking for you. I cut off the light, locked the door and closed it before I locked up the crib and made sure everyone but your friend left." Olivia saying that had put my mind at ease. I thought to myself 'good, at least I didn't do no crazy shit'. "My friend? Who Chanel?" I asked as I walked through the doors of the master bedroom. "Nah that girl Naomi I think that was her name. She was visiting from Texas." Before she could finish her sentence, I already had the answer to the question because Naomi was sound asleep in the bed. "Well, I just wanted to thank you for everything last night you really made it happen for me!"

"Girl no problem, I'm glad you enjoyed yourself! Aren't you flying out to Vegas today?" Olivia asked. "Yeah, my ass need to be getting my shit together I already overslept." I was shaking my head as I made my way into the bathroom of the master bedroom. "Well go ahead and handle ya business, let me know when you make it to Vegas, I may be out there this weekend." Olivia insisted before we ended the call.

I started the shower before walking back into the room to wake Naomi, who was knocked out cold. "Rise and shine!" I said, jumping up on the bed. Naomi pulled the covers over her head, "Nooo, what time is it?" She whined. "Girl it's already noon, our flight leaves in 4 hours so we gotta get going." I said, snatching the covers off of her, before plopping down on the bed next to her laughing. "Girl last night was crazy, you disappeared on me. You must've been lit." She'd finally sat up on the bed and was rubbing the sleep from her eyes. "Girl hell yeah, I was so lit I passed out in the guest room before the party was even over." I laughed as I jumped back off the bed. "I'm bout to hop in the shower, let's get a move on it so we can stop and grab some breakfast I'm starving."

I undressed and brushed my teeth before I hopped in the steaming hot shower. I heard Naomi enter the bathroom, playing one of Lil Saint's newest hits from her cell phone, before she began brushing her teeth. "What we doing when we land? I may have to stop at the mall or something when we get there, I was packed for y'all bi polar ass Georgia weather not Vegas bitch." She called out with a laugh. "Yeah, that's cool, I'm always down to shop but I doubt Saint gone come with us. I really don't know what he has planned for the night though." I was lathering my body with my Dove body wash when I heard the shower door open. I looked back and Naomi was standing there butt ass naked with a wash cloth in her hand. "Mind if I join you? "She asked with a smirk as she stepped inside and closed the door.

She walked up on me as I turned to face her before using her wash cloth to wash my breast. The hot shower water was splashing on my back and that mixed with the breast massage I was receiving had me extremely relaxed and horny. She began to kiss me as she pushed her breasts against mine, causing us to both fall through the streaming water onto the shower wall. She got down on her knees and began to give me head as the water from the shower ran over her. I leaned my head back against the wall and enjoyed the head I was receiving while I ran my hands through her wet hair. After I came on her tongue she stood up and sucked on my breasts for a moment before she continued kissing me. I returned the favor before we finished bathing.

When we arrived in Vegas Saint had a private car pick us up from the airport before taking us to Nobu Hotel where we were escorted through the service elevator up to Saint's suite. Once we got to his door the security knocked on the door to announce our arrival as the bellhop stood behind with our luggage. After a few seconds a short female with huge breasts and long faux locks that ended right above her shapely hips opened the door. I laughed a bit as I brushed past her and Naomi and I made our way inside the suite. Once inside there were about 4 other females and a few of Saint's homeboys standing around, talking, laughing and sipping on drinks.

"Hey baby, happy birthday again I got something for you." Saint grabbed my hand and I followed him into the bedroom where the bed was covered in gifts. There were bags from Gucci, Louis Vuitton, Tiffany, Louboutin shoe boxes, a Rolex and a stack of money right in the middle of it. I covered my face as I smiled in shock that he was spoiling me so good. I mean he was pretty tight on his money so I just enjoyed it for what it was and dropped down to my knees in front of him and thanked him the best way I knew how.

That night Saint had a club appearance and Naomi and I were seated in his section as they popped bottles and rapped along with the DJ's set. "Girl everybody in here tonight!" Naomi stated as she looked around the packed club. "Hell yeah, it's definitely a star-studded occasion. Let's take some shots!" I was ready to get drunk because the way Saint's entourage was bringing bitches into the section, I already knew he was bringing some hoes back to the room. Naomi and I danced on each other and took shots for about two hours before security came to escort us back to the sprinter we were riding in to the next destination.

To true Lil Saint fashion he'd collected two randoms to join us and instead of going to the wild ass mansion after party with everyone else Saint was ready to retire to the hotel. The two random females were all over him as we rode back to the hotel. He'd sparked up a blunt while the caramel skin toned female got in-between his legs and began to give him head while Naomi and I watched. The lighter one of the duo was rubbing her hands through Saint's dreadlocks while he blew her a shot gun. I could tell Naomi was turned on because she was giggling as she stared in my eyes and slid her hand up my dress.

We were all so wasted and horny by the time we made it up the service elevator and into the suite that we were going at it right there in the living room, all five of us. The next morning, I awakened, butt naked, from a buzzing sound and got up off the living room floor thinking maybe it was my phone. I couldn't find my phone for shit but I followed the buzzing sound that seemed to be continuous. I made my way towards the bathroom inside the second room of the suite and shockingly my eyes were met with the most disgusting thing I'd ever seen. Right there, live in living muthafuckin color, was Lil Saint bent over the side of the garden tub as Naomi fucked him with a vibrating dildo.

I covered my mouth before my breath could escape, quietly backing out of the doorway and shutting the door back. I couldn't believe my own eyes as my mind attempted to make sense of what I'd just seen. I mean I knew Saint was into some freaky shit but I never pegged him to be a bottom, no pun intended. I made my way back out of the bedroom and into the main suite to take a shower.

I decided I wouldn't say shit and just act like I'd never seen anything. Naomi and I ended up going shopping while Saint went to the studio. I guess since Naomi knew his little secret, he was not being stingy anymore because he'd handed me his credit card and told us to enjoy Vegas. After hours of burning up his credit card in the hottest stores we made our way back to the hotel to put our new merchandise up before going to grab something to eat at the hotel restaurant.

"Girl you ok? You been kind of quiet all day, something on ya mind?" Naomi asked as we were seated at our table. "Girl yeah I just feel kind of tired. From my wild ass birthday party to flying out here and last night? A bitch is tired ya hear me?" I said with a laugh. "Yeah, well last night was most def some wild shit. I had to watch them hoes though cause you know these bitches be stealing!" Naomi agreed. "Right, he stay bringing these random hoes with us I'm used to that shit at this point." Naomi looked as if she wanted to respond but the waitress came back to the table to take our orders and thankfully changed the direction of the conversation.

CHAPTER NINE

"Bitch have you been on Facebook?" I heard my best friend Latasha scream into the phone. "What? What are you talking about you, why?"

"Bitch them hoes done made a post about you with some list that claims you slept with half the niggas in Atlanta."

"WHAT?! What hoes? What are you talking about?" I was genuinely confused as to what or who she was referring to. On top of that I was still dealing with all my thoughts on Lil Saint ghosting me. "Bitch get on Facebook, Chanel and them done made a post that has gone viral with your pictures all on it." I quickly snatched the phone from my ear and put Latasha on speaker and tapped the Facebook icon on my home screen. I didn't have to search for the post because I had 1,000s of notifications from the post Chanel made of me. I clicked on the post and looked on in horror as I scrolled through pictures of two girls going down on me the night of my birthday party. I recognized them as Chanel's friends and instantly felt sick to my stomach. My eyes read over the comments of people from my home town dragging my name.

The list they put out named a bunch of men that only Chanel knew I'd been with but, to my surprise, she didn't list King. My mouth was wide open as I felt the tears begin to roll down my face. "Girl I told you not to go out there with some hoes you didn't know, now they claiming you basically an escort Moon, what are you gonna do?" Latasha asked me concerned. I was so embarrassed I just wanted to get off the phone with her. "I'm about to take a ride. I'll call you later Tasha thank you for telling me." She was silent for a moment before responding, "Moon call me back for real you know you never do!"

"I got you." I assured her, "I love you Moon." She said as I ended the call. I was so hurt and confused as to why Chanel would betray me on that level. I dialed her number and her trifling ass actually picked up, with a chest full of laughter she says, "Hello?" I gritted my teeth as I attempted to control my emotions before I answered, "Chanel, what the actual fuck?" I couldn't help it I began yelling as I continued, "How you gone expose me on some shit YOU taught me? You been fucking fucking and got the nerve to try to expose me?" I began wiping the tears from my face as she spoke. "I'm sorry, who is this?" I could tell she was laughing and that pissed me all the way off. "Bitch you know exactly who this is!"

"Oh no sweetie I don't know who the fuck this is. See the bitch that I upgraded from a lame ass shoe salesperson to a kept bitch, the bitch I let sleep in my house and fed and clothed until she got on her feet in a new city. Yeah, the bitch that I let into my world with no questions asked, you see THAT bitch would never do me how you did. So again I ask, who is this?" Her tone was very calm as she spoke and it was making my blood boil. "What are you even talking about? I've never did anything but be loyal to you! I took your shit for the last 3 years, you're talking sideways to me, treating me and everyone around you like we ain't shit! I had to put up with your nasty ass attitude and your controlling behavior but you think I somehow betrayed you? On the level that warranted THIS response?"

"The fact that you can still sit here and act like you oh so innocent lets me know you're exactly who you exposed yourself to be, everything you just said about me describes you to a T. You're a narcissistic, selfish ass, ungrateful ass little girl. King told me everything, how you were heavy on his line behind my back, asking for gifts and reporting back to him on me and shit. Bitch you fucked up and now everyone else knows it!" Chanel began laughing a sinister laugh before continuing, "Matter of fact, send me 25K and I'll take the post down." She ended the call as she continued to laugh in my ear.

I paced back and forth in my living room as I kept trying to contact Saint. He'd given me $50,000 cash for my birthday and Chanel had me fucked up if she thought I was giving her half. I was down to my last $10,000 in my accounts and I needed every penny I had. I sat down on my Italian leather couch and bit on my bottom lip as I tried to calm my mind so I could think clearly. My phone began to ring and I saw Olivia's face pop up on my screen. I quickly answered the phone hoping she had heard from Saint.

"Hey girl." I said dryly. "Hey love, did I catch you at a bad time? I was calling to see how your weekend in Sin City went!" From her response I knew she hadn't heard about him ghosting me or this viral post Chanel had made of me. "I mean the trip was cool but I came back home to some bull shit!" I revealed to her as I walked into my kitchen to pour myself a glass of wine. "Girl what the hell done happened?" She asked. "You on Facebook?" I asked as I pulled the app back up.

"Yeah, what's up?"

"Olivia the girls I moved down here took advantage of me the night of my birthday. I mean they had to have drugged me because I don't remember shit but they have pictures of me passed out in my birthday dress while two chicks went down on me." Olivia gasped as I continued. "They made up a list of people I supposedly slept with and the shit done went viral. To make matters worse I think Saint was sent the post and he has blocked me on everything and is ghosting me!" I finally felt the tears as I cried silently, downing the entire glass of wine I'd poured as the reality of the situation set in.

"What? Why would chicks you consider friends do this to you?" She asked with concern. "I don't know, jealousy probably. They were mad I was getting serious with Saint." I shook my head as I poured another glass of wine before I paced back and forth in my kitchen, thinking. "Well, you will learn in this game you don't really have friends only connections. Send me the post and I'll get it taken care of. As far as Saint, I can't lie to you if he saw the post or was sent information on you, he will not continue to pursue you, he's filled with too much pride." She admitted to me. I felt relieved that she was willing to help me but I was sick to my stomach thinking about losing Saint.

It took her all of 13 hours but Olivia got the post removed from Facebook and got Chanel's social media accounts banned for harassment. I knew that even though the post had been removed my reputation was not going to be able to be salvaged back in my hometown. My father texting me a long message letting me know that I'd shamed the family yet again was proof of that. At this point I had to embrace the title they gave me. If I was a hoe, I was gonna be a paid hoe!

One week later I was in Los Angeles with Olivia taking a well needed break from the chaos surrounding the viral post. The basketball players that were funding our weekend was throwing a yacht party and I was so ready to get a new roster. Olivia had introduced me to two of her female friends, Alana and Megan, traveling with us and we all clicked instantly. I had my phone out to flex for the gram when the baller I'd been crushing all day finally came over to break the ice. "Damn lil momma why I never seen you out in LA before?" He asked as he bit into the slice of pineapple that he'd taken off the side of my glass. I smiled at him, "That's because before I didn't have a reason to come out here." I said in a sultry tone. "Well, I gotta change that, come give me a dance." He said, grabbing my hand and pulling me towards him.

I spun around and placed my drink on the ground before bending over and making my ass clap, dipping low, backing up against his rising penis and twerking on him until he was at full attention. He grabbed my waist and pulled me into him as he grinded against me. The boat was lit so everyone was in their own zone when he whispered in my ear, "Touch it." I grinned before turning to face him, looking him directly in the eyes and slowly stuffing my hand down his swim trunks and gripping his huge dick. I squeezed and pulled as we stared into each other eyes, he was biting on his bottom lip and I kept going until he came into my hand. "Oh shit." He let out, pulling me close to him, as he regained his composure. I winked at him and pulled my hand from inside his swimming trunks, hand filled with his semen. "I'll be back." I told him with a smile.

I made my way below deck and found the bathroom before washing my hands and staring at myself in the mirror. I looked good as fuck in my Gucci two piece and just had to get a quick picture for the Gram. I pulled my phone out of my Gucci fanny pack before posing in the mirror until I got the right shot. I heard the door open behind me and Olivia was making her way inside with me. "What the fuck was that?" She asked me, crossing her arms in front of her chest. "What was what?" I asked, confused. "Bitch don't play with me. I saw you and that nigga up there! I hope you charged him for that nut." She said as she walked up on me and fixed my misplaced hair. I laughed before responding, mostly from embarrassment. "I mean I got caught up in the moment shit I'm drunk as fuck."

"Well bitch drink water cause that's not the type of chick I allow around me. If you gone fuck that's fine but you never do that shit for free you understand me?" I didn't respond verbally I just shook my head in agreement. "Turn around." She instructed me to face the mirror as she stood beside me. "You are beautiful, those freckles, those eyes and this body is worth a nigga running his pockets. Teasing is cool but remember the point of the tease. If you trust me and let me guide you on how to really be in this world, I will quadruple your pockets in less than 6 months. But the more niggas you let sample this," She put her hands inside my bikini bottom, as we both looked at each other in the mirror.

"The less valuable it becomes." She began to swirl her fingers around my clit before pushing them inside me. "Wha what are you doing?" I asked as I began to moan. "Cum for me since you so horny, relax and enjoy it." My breathing picked up as she fingered me until I creamed on her fingers. She pulled her hand out with a smile and washed her hands before we walked out the bathroom together and made our way back to the top where the party was still going on.

The party was being thrown by a very well professional basketball player, we will call him Dade Wayne, and his actress wife. There were seven other pro ball players in attendance but we will leave them out of it because they aren't really important for this part of the story. The yacht we were on was extravagant to say the least. There were three levels to the boat and on the main deck, where everyone was mingling, there was a huge hot tub, dance floor, full bar, a diving board and slide that lead off the side of the boat into the ocean, and a huge covered seating area. The shit was niccceee!

When we made it back up, I noticed that the basketball player that I'd jacked off just fifteen minutes earlier was whispering sweet nothings in another chick's ear. I couldn't help but laugh and shake my head before making my way over to the bar with Olivia, "Shit, I left my phone in the bathroom I'll be right back." Olivia said, not waiting for my response before making her way back towards the doors that lead downstairs. I vibed to the music as the bartender made the lemon drop I'd requested. While waiting I got the shock of my life when Dade Wayne's wife walked up to me.

"I've never seen you around before, you're Olivia's friend, right? I'm Giselle." She held her hand out and I accepted it, "Yeah Olivia is my girl, I'm Moon, nice to meet you." She bit her bottom lip as if she were thinking of something before responding, "Are you out here for the entire weekend?" She asked. "Yeah, we leave Monday afternoon." She raised her hand to the bar tender and he turned and began making a drink. "Well, you have to come out with us, if Olivia vouches for you, I know you're good. Give me your number."

Now I had seen this woman is several movies growing up and even her own TV show that happened to be one of my favorites. I couldn't believe I was in her presence let alone being asked for my number. Of course, I didn't hesitate to give her my number. I mean these people are paid! Just as the bartender was placing her drink in front of her Naomi was walking back up with her phone in her hand. "Hey Giselle, I meant to tell you I love this bathing suit girl! 43 where honey?" Olivia laughed as she looked Giselle up and down. "Thank you, girl, I saw this in Fendi and knew I had to have it. I was just talking to your girl here, she's beautiful." She said, swirling her straw around her drink before taking a sip. I didn't know if I was tripping or not but Gisselle was giving off crazy masculine energy. "Yeah, ain't she? She just turned 21 too." Olivia said with a sly grin.

Gisselle's eyebrow raised as she diverted her attention back to me. "21? Well, that means you're old enough to party." She said with a wink before smacking Olivia gently on her ass and walking off. "I must be damn dreaming or something cause what just happened?" I asked with a laugh. "Oh

Gisselle? Yeah, she and Dade are down with the get down so if she feeling you don't forget to get that bag." She raised her glass for me to toast with her. "To having one life, and living that muthafuckin to the fullest!" I hit my cup against hers and we both downed the entire contents of our glasses before ordering another round and making our way back over to the party.

After we ate dinner the yacht took us back to dock where me, Olivia and her two homegirls hopped in the back of the private car waiting for us. We rode back to the Air Bnb mostly in silence because we were all exhausted and just wanted to get some rest. When we got back in Alana and Megan both went to their separate rooms, stumbling drunk, while Olivia pulled me into her room to talk. We both sat on the bed and kicked off our shoes before she began, "Did you enjoy yourself today?" She asked as she opened the drawer on the nightstand and pulled out a Victoria Secret bag. "I want you to put this on and let me take some pictures of you." Her request was kind of weird to me but I was beyond tipsy and I was feeling myself so I said fuck it and grabbed the bag before starting to make my way to the bathroom.

"Where you going?" She asked me in a serious tone. I looked back at her, confusion obvious on my face. "I'm going to put it on."

"Nah, get undressed right there." I shrugged my shoulders and dropped the bag, taking off my Gucci swim suit cover up. "Slow down, I want you to give me a show, do it like you wanna fuck me." She instructed. I didn't respond before slowing down and seductively swaying my hips as I un tied my swim suit top and freeing my breasts as Olivia pulled her phone out and began snapping pictures of me. I trusted her so I didn't mind as I continued my sexy striptease. I turned around as I slowly took stepped out of my bikini bottom, giving her a full view of my perfect ass. I bent down and pulled out the red lacy lingerie with the matching red, see-through, robe. I continued to dance to my own beat in my head as I stepped into the one piece before slowly putting on the robe as I walked towards her seated on the bed, with her back against the backboard, still snapping photos of me. "Lay down." She told me as I reached her. I got on the bed and laid on my back before Olivia climbed on top of me and began taking my picture from above me.

I gave her my best fuck me faces while she

cheered me on with compliments and your occasional, "Yasss, show me you want me to fuck you!" At this point I wanted to feel her tongue on my wet opening but shockingly she just stopped, got off of me, and said "You did good, go get you some sleep we got a long day tomorrow." I couldn't help the confused look on my face as I closed the gown and slid off the bed, embarrassed. "Ok, I guess I'll see you in the morning." I said, gathering my things off of the floor and making my way towards the door. "Yeah, hit the lights for me and close my door on your way out if you don't mind." I quietly did as I was asked while walking out of her room.

The next day I got up and the first thing I did was check my phone. It had been a few weeks since my birthday weekend and I still hadn't heard from Saint. I had hope that one day, especially with how close Olivia and I were getting, we'd run into each other again. I got out of the bed and made my way in the bathroom to get ready for the day before making my way downstairs. When I entered the kitchen Olivia's friend, Alana, was seated on one of the barstools in front of the marble island countertop on facetime with some guy. "Good morning, you look cute." She said, looking over at me as I opened the fridge to look for some juice. "Thank you girl, I didn't know what was on the agenda for the day so I kept it cute comfy." I'd decided on a pair of red Gucci shorts, a tight, white, baby tee with Gucci stitched in red across my breasts. I topped it off with my white Gucci sneakers and my Gucci hat.

"Yeah, I think we going shopping and then to some restaurant Olivia was talking about. But I have a date later on with one of the ballers from last night." She revealed, after ending her facetime call with the player, who shall remain nameless, she was referring to. Just then, Olivia joined us in the kitchen rocking a brown and black Fendi romper with a pair of black Fendi slides, and she was icy per usual. "Good morning ladies!" she sang as she stood next me on the opposite side of the island from Alana. "Good morning girl, I love this romper. Alana was just telling me what you had planned for us today." I told her as I leaned against the counter top and grabbed one of the fresh oranges from the blue porcelain bowl in the center of the counter and began peeling it. "Alana, why don't you go get Megan, let her know we're about to head out."

Alana hopped off the barstool and made her

way out of the kitchen as Olivia turned towards me, pulling a piece of paper out of her pocket and handing it to me. "You're going to go to this address and tell them you want a full screening done on rush. You're going to wait there until you get your results back and then you call me. There is a car already waiting for you outside." She didn't wait on my response before she pulled her shades down from her pink hair and putting them over her eyes and turning to walk away.

I felt so awkward seated in the waiting room of the clinic Olivia had sent me to as I filled out the paperwork on the clear clipboard. I hadn't been to a gynecologist, nor been tested since I turned 18 and I can't lie I was nervous as fuck. When the older white lady behind the receptionist desk called my name, I walked up to give her my ID and she looked at me before asking, "Have you finished the paperwork? They are ready for you." I handed her back the clipboard, "Yes, I'm done." She grabbed it from me and said, "Good, the nurse will call you back shortly." She went back to doing whatever she was up to on her computer before I walked back to my seat and waited for the nurse.

The four hours I waited at the clinic drug by as my stomach growled and I grew bored of scrolling through all of my social media. Lucky for me I had a clean bill of health and I was dialing Olivia's number to share the news. When she answered she told me that they'd just sat down to eat and she was sending a car to pick me up. I arrived at the restaurant 35 minutes later and the three of them were seated in a booth enjoying cocktails and appetizers as they waited on me. "Hey ladies! Did y'all miss me?" I asked as I slid into the booth next to Olivia. "Hell yeah, we saw a gang of celebrities today on Rodeo drive. Shit was lit, we starving though." Megan said as she grabbed a tortilla chip and dipped it in the bowl of hot spinach dip they'd ordered.

"Yeah, we were waiting on you to get here but we already know what we want." Olivia said as she handed me a menu. "So, what were y'all talking about?" I asked as I looked over the menu. "Oh, nothing really, Alana was telling about the Black Lives Matter marches she attended after this last shooting in Texas of the teenager Jordan Edwards." Olivia informed me. "Oh word? Wow, my brother was actually killed by the police four and a half months ago on February 3rd, he didn't get much news coverage though." I stated, attempting to sound as sad as I could. In actuality I didn't think of MJ much, I'd put everything involving my family and hometown inside a box and locked it away. Honestly, looking back on it, I was too ashamed to face them after Chanel blasted my business on Facebook.

"Damn, I didn't know that! I'm so sorry to hear that." Oliva said as she placed a hand on my shoulder. "Yeah, it's not something I can really deal with talking about but I'm glad to know I'm around people who are fighting to stop it from happening to another family." I was relieved when the waitress walked back up to the table to take our orders. We didn't really talk about anything in particular at lunch but when Olivia and I said our goodbye's to Alana and Megan, who both had dates, and got into the private car together that's when the conversation got interesting. "I spoke to Gisselle earlier today and she wanted you to come to her house for a private party, are you down?" She asked me as she looked down into her phone.

"Are you kidding? Hell yeah, I'm down! What you gonna wear?" I asked her excitedly. "Oh, I wouldn't be joining you; it would just be the three of you."

"But I thought Megan and Alana were going

out tonight?" I asked, confused. "Yeah, they are, I mean the three of you, as in you, Gisselle and Dade. I mean Moon do I have to spell this out for you?" She asked as she finally looked up at me from her phone. I raised an eyebrow before she continued. "They are paying $20,000 for the night and of course 5000 of that will go to me."

"Wait what?

"Which part are you confused on?" Olivia asked. "The part that involves me giving you $5,000 off my pussy." I responded with a laugh. "Moon look, you are getting this offer off my face card alone. You stick with me you'll always have money flowing. Do you trust me?" She asked as she stared me in my eyes. "I mean yeah I trust you, I just didn't know how it worked, I guess. That's all." I mean it made sense so I decided not to get too worked up over it. Besides, I would get to fuck Dade Wayne and Gisselle! My pussy got wet just thinking about it. Olivia was giving me the run-down of what to expect once I got to their home in the hills but nothing could've prepared me for the evening I had ahead of me.

After getting dressed in the black leather dress and 6-inch, open-toe Valentino stilettos

Olivia had purchased for me I was picked up by a black SUV and taken to the hills. I was stopped at the gate and asked to sign an NDA and I had to leave my cell phone and purse with security before the driver was allowed through the gate. At this point I'd been around my fair share of "elite" so it was routine to have to sign an NDA when entering some of their homes.

Once the driver came around and let me out of the truck I was met at the front door by a female butler. "Good evening madam, the Wayne's are waiting for you in the kitchen, right this way." I stepped to the side as she closed the huge door and followed her through the foyer into the kitchen where Giselle was dancing to the R&B music they had playing through their home's built-in speakers. Dade was eating a bowl of mixed fruit as he egged her on. "Mr. and Mrs. Wayne, your company has arrived. If that is all I will be leaving now." The butler announced before bowing and turning to make her exit. "Hey!" Giselle, who had obviously been drinking, exclaimed as she walked over towards me to give me a hug. "Damn you look good in that dress girl, I'm sure you know my husband, baby this is Moon." She introduced us as she rubbed her hands through my hair.

"Hey Moon, come make yourself comfortable." He said, pulling out one of the tall chairs at the table. "Can I get you anything to drink? We about to take some shots." Giselle said as she made her way to the fridge. "You have any orange juice or cranberry?" I asked, taking a seat as Dade Wayne rubbed the inside of my thigh with the outside of his hand, instantly sending a chill up my spine. "We have both!" She said as she pulled them out. "I'll take orange juice then."

"You not from around here are you?" Dade asked me as he made his way behind me to begin massaging my shoulders. "No, I'm from Missouri but I live in Atlanta. Both are only one flight away." I said as Giselle joined us with a bottle of Cîroc a few cups and a carafe of orange juice. "I like this one, she's quick on her feet." Dade said to his wife as he continued massaging me. "Yeah, I knew you'd like her, I can't wait to lick her freckles." She said with a wink, causing me to smile.

We took shots and enjoyed casual conversation that we ended up taking to their huge living room. They were actually pretty dope people in my opinion. After about an hour and a half of talking and drinking Giselle began getting very flirty and touchy before she began kissing me while she straddled me on their couch, as Dade watched. I fondled her breasts through her bra as we kissed passionately and got so lost in her passion that I didn't even see Dade get completely undressed and sit down on the couch next to us. Giselle suddenly pulled my head back by my hair and said, "I want you to use that tongue on him while I watch." She said, kissing me one more time before getting off my lap.

I stood up and got down on my knees in front of him and began massaging his dick with both my hands, spitting on it, until I had him at full attention and took him whole into my watering, warm mouth. He moaned out as I massaged his balls with one of my hands as I used the other to twist up and down on his shaft as I pleased him with the back of my throat. Giselle watched as she fingered herself until she couldn't take it anymore. "Ok, that's good, now let's take it to the champagne room." She said as she pulled my head out of his lap.

The champagne room was a room in the lower level of their home that was all red with a huge, black Tufted upholstered platform bed, a sex swing, full bar and a huge black armoire on the opposite side of the room. It was barely lit with sexy red lights and there were no paintings or anything else decorating the room. "Strip." Giselle demanded as Dade hopped up on the bed. I did as I was asked while she walked over to the armoire, opening it and revealing its contents. There were several whips, chains handcuffs, blindfolds, dildos, strap-ons and more. She took off her robe and pulled out one of the whips before cracking it against the floor as I stepped out of my dress. "Leave the heels on and join him in the bed." She instructed me. I walked over to join Dade on the bed, who was lying back against the headboard, rubbing his erect penis in anticipation.

"Lay down." I heard Giselle's voice demand from across the room. I complied as I watched Dade sit up and get in-between my legs, wrapping them around his neck as he began to eat me out. Swirling his tongue over my clit before inserting it in and out of my dripping pussy. I rubbed my hands over his waves as I witnessed Giselle walk up behind him, with a strap-on on her crotch, and entered Dade from behind. He began going wild on my pussy, sucking and spitting my juices back inside me as he continued to make me nut back back-to-back. He finally came up for air and moaned as he exploded onto the bed from the pegging Giselle was pleasing him with.

Giselle joined me on the bed, after stepping out of the strap-on, and replaced Dade's mouth with her own. She inserted two of her fingers inside of me as she licked and sucked on my clit. Dade was entering her from behind as she bent over with her face between my legs and her ass in the air. I couldn't believe I was fucking two of the most famous celebrities in the world but I was definitely enjoying every minute of it. I squirted in her mouth as she pulled me up to suck on her breasts while Dade wrapped a hand around her neck, choking her slightly as he continued to drive his dick inside of her wet opening.

I licked on her breasts and gave her nipples a lot of attention as I slightly nibbled and pinched on them as I twirled my tongue over her juicy breasts. She was moaning in pleasure and it was turning me on. I wanted some of his dick for myself! I looked Dade in his eyes as I took two of my fingers and pushed them inside his ass while I continued to suck on Giselle's breasts. He began fucking the shit out of her as I teased him and found his G-spot. It didn't take him but 10 seconds to climax again, this time inside his wife. He stayed inside her for a moment as he caught his breath before letting out a laugh and smacking her on her round brown ass watching it jiggle before they both laid down on the bed.

It was time for me to return the favor and of course I had to show out since I knew I wanted this to happen again especially with the bag they were playing with. I started with Dade as I licked the tip of his flaccid penis and watched it jump. I knew exactly what would get him at full attention so I said fuck it and lifted his dick and licked his asshole. He clinched a bit at first but he relaxed and I went to work as I massaged his dick back awake and licked his ass. He was moaning as Giselle got behind me and began to do the same to me. Eating my pussy and licking my ass from behind as she stuck a finger in my ass. I was in complete ecstasy as I began cumming hard, squirting hard on their expensive sheets. "Baby, she's definitely a squirter, come give her what she's been waiting for." She instructed her husband who quickly obliged, pulling me up from his ass and flipping me around towards him. He entered me from behind and I began gripping him to pull him in as he pulled my hair back and began picking up the pace.

Giselle got out of the bed and began watching me and her husband fuck in all different types of positions; I even let them put me in their sex swing since I'd never been in one before. We fucked for hours before we all passed out from exhaustion. I awakened the next morning to the Butler handing me my clothes and a "Thank you" Bag and informing me that I had 20 minutes to get up and dressed and outside for the car waiting to take me back to my Air BnB.

When I got back to the spot everyone was either still asleep or not back yet but I was still drained so I went straight to my room to get some more sleep. I wasn't asleep long because next thing I knew Olivia was waking me up, "So did you enjoy yourself last night?" She asked me as she snatched the covers from over my head and plopped down on the bed next to me. "Oh my god! What time is it? I'm exhausted." I whined as I attempted to pull the covers back up. "Girl take you a goody's powder and drink you a Red Bull, cause it's already after one and we have shit to do today. The other girls just got back and are getting ready, I got us a chef who is preparing lunch for us today he downstairs now." Olivia said as she snatched the covers off of me again.

I whined as I sat up reluctantly, "I got your money right here, they put that shit in a thank you bag." I said with a laugh before reaching over on the night stand and handing Olivia her portion of the money. "Remember when you asked me what I did for a living outside of real estate?" She asked as she looked over at me with a straight face. "Yeah?" I answered as I scrunched my face in confusion. "Well, I'm what is considered in the industry a high-profile madam. I find girls like you and I hook you up with the elite men who pay top dollar for discretion and sexual freedom. I have to tell you something and I don't want you to take it personal." She took a deep breath before she continued. "The girl you introduced me to at your birthday, Naomi I think, she and Saint have been dating ever since you took her out there that weekend." I couldn't believe it but I also couldn't be mad either. I was beginning to understand how the game worked and it was never supposed to be about feelings. Besides, it made sense, seeing as though I hadn't heard from her ass since that weekend either.

I fucked up when I brought another bitch in on my situation and since I walked in on her fucking him with a dildo, I knew it was because she was willing to do the same shit I felt was nasty until I experienced it with Giselle and Dade. I mean I was sure that these powerful men had so much sex given to them over the years that they had to eventually grow tired of just regular sex with regular women. I had decided in the Wayne's champagne room that I was willing to do whatever it took to secure a bag. If that meant I never had to see St. Louis Missouri ever again.

"Yeah, I ain't tripping off that, I fumbled that bag. But I'm trying to hear more about this madam shit you were talking about." I was curious to know how she could help me get the men with the real money so I never had to work again. "Moon I'm very connected and well respected, I don't take what I do lightly and I can't have any liabilities on my hands. Yesterday was a test and even though you almost fucked up with that stunt you pulled on the yacht you came through and still secured the bag. If I bring you on my roster you will belong to me, and I don't mean that in any other way than exactly how it sounds. I get 30% of everything you make and you don't do any freelance dating or fucking at all. If I ever find out that you fucked someone outside of your clients, I will drop you and you won't ever get another booking through me again. If you are ok with that then I'll see you downstairs in 30 minutes for lunch on the back lawn, if not you can pack your things and head back to Atlanta." Olivia got out of the bed and adjusted her dress before making her way out of the room with her cash in her hands.

I didn't have to think at all about joining her team, I was down when she told me she only dealing with elite men. I was cool with that; I mean I was only 21 so it wasn't like I wanted to get married anytime soon anyway. I got dressed and made my way downstairs to where I could smell the aroma of something delicious being cooked in the kitchen. The ladies were all seated at the table as they drank wine and talked about their dates from the day before. "Bitch his dick was so small I was surprised he even attempted to put a condom on!" Alana laughed as she drank her wine. "What y'all crazy asses in here talking about?" I joined them at the table as Olivia poured me a glass of wine.

CHAPTER TEN

I'd only been working with Olivia for 6 months and already had been with over 75 men. Most of them I was fucking on the regular but a few I'd never seen again. I was being flown all over the world by all types of rich ass men and I didn't discriminate. I had fucked Spanish men, Asian men, Italian men, white men, and even Indian men. But nothing prepared me for the experience that began on this day in December of 2017. My day started off like any typical day, I woke up around noon and got on my phone to check all my social media, mostly to see how many likes and comments my last post of me got from before stepping out to the club the night before. I was rocking a lime green strapless dress with a pair of nude stilettos with a clear heel and my clear YSL clutch. My hair was in a high, drastic, 40-inch pony tail and the 100,000+ likes I'd received only confirmed what I already knew, I was "That Bitch."

I checked my email after spending half an hour on IG and I saw I had an email from Olivia. I opened it immediately and began reading it over.

Agent 1475

Date: Friday December 29 2017- Monday January 1st 2018

Location: Dubai

Description of job: Accompany a variety of clients to; and after holiday festivities.

Offer: $100,000 plus travel and wardrobe.

If you accept this offer you understand that the agreement gives the client COMPLETE control over your contract and it's stipulations. In the acceptance response letter please add your measurements and there will be an NDA sent to you once your full bloodwork screening is updated and returned within 48 hours.

THIS MESSAGE IS TO BE DELETED UPON RECIEPT

I read the whole message and wrote down as much information as I saw necessary before deleting the email and removing it from my trash bin. I knew that with a pay day of $100,000 these had to be some freaky ass clients. I figured it would be some orgy type shit but I didn't give a fuck! I was going to muthafuckin DUBAI bitch!

I'd seen all the IG models I looked up to going to Dubai and I was excited that it was my turn. I was about to make 100K just to fuck some freaky ass niggas, I was down! I quickly responded with my acceptance of the job and called the doctor's office to get my appointment in.

Two weeks later I was being dropped off at a big ass mansion in Buckhead with my Gucci luggage. I was greeted at the door by Olivia who was smiling from ear to ear as she gave me a hug. "Hey girl, you're looking and smelling good. You ready for that 16-hour flight?" She asked me as I rolled my bags in and she closed the door. "Hell yeah! I'm ready to see Dubai and stunt for the gram one time." I said with a laugh. "You can leave your bags here and follow me, the other girls you're traveling with are in the dining room having mimosas."

We walked through the kitchen into the dining room and there were three girls seated at the table drinking and talking to one another. One of the girls was a blonde white girl with huge breasts, the other was a brown skin curvy chick with sandy blonde naturally curly hair and the final female was an Indian girl with long jet-black hair and a thin frame. They were all drop dead gorgeous.

After Olivia made introductions between myself and the three girls, Strawberry, Mocha and Jasmyn we all got to know each other for a moment before Olivia raised her glass to get our attention. Once the room fell completely silent Olivia began, "Well ladies I know for Strawberry and Jasmyn this is all routine for you at this point but this will be the first Dubai trip for Moon and Mocha. Each of you have received the emails informing you of certain Dubai customs that you must abide by and I appreciate you all for abiding by the dress code lined out for travel. Moon and Mocha the clients you all are about to meet have peculiar taste and things may get a little crazy but remember they have full control and you agreed to the anything goes clause. If you are not feeling comfortable this is the final chance to back out, once you receive this money you are agreeing to all terms. Do you all understand?" Olivia asked as she stood in front of us sipping her mimosa.

We all agreed again before she continued, "If you haven't checked by now $20,000 was transferred into your accounts this morning, I've already received my 30%. You each will receive the remainder of your $50,000 payment only after you return to the states. If you ladies have no questions the limo is pulling up outside to take you to the airport now."

We each looked at each other and to be real all of us had money on our mind so we all raised our glasses to toast before downing the remainder of our drinks and getting up to head out the front door where the driver was already loading our luggage into the back of an SUV while we hopped inside the limo. One of the girls, Strawberry, wasted no time popping the champagne waiting in the ice bucket as we pulled out of the driveway. I was snapping videos of the ride as we turned up like we were the best of friends. The 16-hour plane ride to Dubai we all slept most of the flight but I was sure to catch the skyline when we were arriving. I couldn't believe how beautiful it was.

The house that we were taken to from the airport was best described as a palace. The men in America had money but the men in Dubai? Oh, they were definitely playin with a different type of bag! When we rode up the long driveway, surrounded by a landscaped garden with mature greenery fit for magazines, I took pictures of everything. I couldn't believe how beautiful the contemporary style home was. The beautiful glass doors and windows all over gave you a view of the main areas of the home from outside. I could see four women dressed in black and gold Abaya's and black headscarves over their heads and faces, only exposing their eyes standing at the front door awaiting our arrival.

When we exited the car, two of the women came down to get our bags while the other two showed us inside. There was music I'd never heard before playing throughout the house as the two women silently walked us up the stairs. "Why they ain't saying shit?" I whispered to the girl Strawberry who had done this before. "Girl they never say shit, they about to take us to our rooms where we will have to change clothes and then they will come back and get us one by one. Be cool, it's always a whole lot of liquor in the rooms. If you want my advice, start drinking now!"

Just as she finished her sentence the ladies stopped abruptly before pointing at Mocha and opening the door to the room she'd be staying in. I was the second to get my room and when I walked in, I was amazed at the decor. They had the most expensive taste I'd ever seen. Even my bed was made out of gold, draped in Italian sheets. I had my own private bathroom with a huge jacuzzi sized tub and a shower fit for 10. You know I had to flex on the Gram so I opened the doors to the balcony connected to my suite and began snapping selfies, being sure to capture the 20-foot-long pool in the backyard of the mansion in my background.

After finally getting the perfect angles I posted the pictures and continued examining the room. There was a clothing rack next to a gold and white marble vanity that had about 15 different outfits on it. I looked through them and chose an orange and gold Abaya before making my way into the bathroom to turn my shower water on. I started playing some music before I stepped out of my clothes and into the hot steaming shower.

After I was done, I walked back into the bedroom and noticed that my bags had been dropped off. I moisturized my body before putting on my sexy black lingerie and stepping into the abaya. I pinned my hair up and put on the jewelry that had been laid out for me before snapping a few more pictures for the Gram and making myself a drink from the mini bar in my room. I was 6 shots in and on my third cup of Hennessey by the time the door to my room opened and one of the ladies came to take me downstairs.

I was escorted downstairs into a huge

entertainment room that had a buffet table filled with fruit and finger foods, a bar equipped with a bartender, while beautiful golden statues and crazy artwork decorated the walls and floors. There were several chairs spread around the room but the nine men in attendance were all standing around the bar smoking on cigars as the music continued to play, completely ignoring our presence. I saw Strawberry and Jasmyn and made my way over to them as I drank from my cup. I took a seat next to them on one of the chairs and asked, "So what now? How do we know which of them is our client?" I wasn't sure why I was whispering but the men we were there with didn't give off friendly vibes so I was just playing it safe.

"Girl just do yourself a favor and drink as much of this free liquor as you can, and stop talking." She said through clinched teeth in a low tone. We were the only women in the home who didn't have our heads covered but it was as if we were just pieces of furniture in the room because the men never looked in our direction not one time as they partied and conversed with one another in Arabic. They carried on for two full hours while we were forced to sit in silence before I witnessed one of the other women come and get Jasmyn and take her out of the room. Ten minutes later the same two women came back and retrieved me to escort me to another room.

The room I was taken to this time wasn't as extravagant as the room I was taken to when I arrived and there was plastic all over the floor of the room. The only furniture in the room was a circle shaped bed covered in a red waterproof bedsheet. It dawned on me that the men must've been into some type of R. Kelly peeing shit. I kept repeating to myself, "$70,000 bitch, $70,000." As I began to undress to lay on the bed. There was no way some Dubai nigga was pissing on my new lingerie so I got butt ass naked and lay across the bed. I was extremely drunk by this time so I was horny and ready for a good fuck.

A few minutes later the door to the room I was in opened and a big hairy guy with a huge belly walked in dressed only in a robe. He didn't say anything to me he came in and got right on top of me, pushing all 4 inches of himself into me, pumping 8 times before pulling out and jacking off onto my face. I went to wipe my face with my hand and he knocked my hand away, "Leave it." He grunted before getting up and walking out of the room. As he made his exit another guy walked in. This one was just as hairy but he was somewhat attractive with a nice body. He flipped me over and rammed his dick in my ass, causing me to scream from the pain. He smashed my face into the bed as he rammed in and out forcefully. I could feel my ass hole ripping but I bit down on my bottom lip and waited for it to be over.

When he was done, he released his seed inside my ass and got up to leave. I was in so much pain as I felt the blood leaking from my ass as it mixed with his semen. I went to turn over and another guy was walking in, untying his robe, exposing his huge dick. His chest was hairy as fuck but unlike the two before him he wasn't hairy anywhere else. He was kind of chubby but not in a sloppy way and I was relieved when he entered my vagina from behind instead of my ass. He screamed at me while he fucked me, calling me bitches and dirty whores while he spit on my back and yanked hard on my hair. Once he was ready to cum, he snatched my head back and forced my mouth open to catch his nut.

He grunted as he released and then pushed my head back down before walking out of the room. This routine went on a few more times but I lost count after him. The liquor I'd consumed had begun to get the best of me and their faces all became a blur so I can't really tell you how many of them fucked me that night. I woke up the next morning naked, sticky and sore. I rolled out of the bed and gathered my clothes, slipping the abaya over my body and balling my lingerie up in my hands and made my way back out to find my room.

I found my original room and went inside to wash the night off of me and get ready for the day. The itinerary I'd received said that we'd be spending the day out on the ocean but we were to wear our abaya's until the yacht sailed out from the dock. I chose a yellow one from the rack that was the closest match to my bikini choice for the day and was dressed and ready to go by noon. I was starving by this time and I was relieved that one of the women had come to retrieve me from the suite and escorted my downstairs to the dining area where there was a 12-foot-long African Blackwood dining table decorated with gold plates and serving trays. The entire table was covered with all different types of foods and I could see that there were two new faces at the table but everyone was quiet as they all ate.

I felt weird not being able to be myself and

talk to the girls that were in the room with me but I didn't wanna fuck up my money so I silently made my plate and sat down at the table, snapping pictures of the food, before digging into the delicious spread.

An hour later we were all boarding the yacht to set out for a 6-hour boat ride. The yacht I was on with Olivia and the Wayne's was big but this? This was almost a mini cruise ship. The boat was huge, they had a huge swimming pool on the lower deck that stretched the entire length of the deck, the pool had a slide and swim up bar, and another slide off the back of the boat that led into the ocean. There was a beautiful elaborate waterfall with sheets of water flowing down a glass partition between the pool and the beach club area. The beach club area, for those who have never been on a yacht before, is basically like a waterside lounge area with fold-down platforms on all three sides to continue the ambiance of being outside while having the comfort of being covered and entertained by the huge flat screen tv and stereo. There was a second bar in this area as well as the view of the glass bottom swimming pool on the aft deck above.

On the aft deck, basically the upper deck,

there was a smaller glass bottom pool and a hot tub fit for 12. Y'all, this yacht had a 6-seat cinema, sauna, spa, full gym and cigar bar. It was like something out of a movie. My pussy got wet just thinking about all the money I was around. I'd found out from Jasmyn, on the ride over to the dock, that the fat guy with the small penis from the night before was the Owner of the house we were staying in. She wasn't sure what he did for a living but she said he was into some nasty shit. I didn't care though if he wanted to pee on my face, call me bad names, use me to please his friends hell it didn't matter to me with the type of money he had.

When we all got on the boat the atmosphere was a lot better than back at the house. The guys were laughing and drinking with us as we all enjoyed the boat's amenities. I was floating in the pool as I enjoyed the sun on my body and face. I'd zoned everything out as I enjoyed the calming sound of the water rolling me, with ease, around the pool. I had a huge smile on my face even though we weren't allowed to bring our phones on the boat. I felt accomplished, I was in Dubai with some of the richest men in the world and I was getting paid to do it.

Me and the girls ended up at the swim-up

bar taking shots as we played the game never have I ever. We were lit as a few of the men made their way into the pool with us to join the game. They were a lot younger than all the other men in attendance and they most definitely weren't there the night before. We all asked outlandish questions and laughed uncontrollably each time someone had to take a shot. I felt a hand in-between my legs rubbing on my clit through my bikini bottom and turned to see one of the guys grinning as I rubbed against his fingers as the game went on. "Let's play truth or dare!" One of the girls, who'd arrived that morning, blurted out with a laugh. "Hell yeah, I'll go first." Strawberry volunteered as the guy finally inserted his fingers inside of me. I was grinding against his hand as I watched Strawberry remove her top after accepting the first dare.

"Come with me." The guy whispered in my ear as I took another shot and followed him out of the pool. We went below deck into one of the open cabins and he wasted no time slipping out of his wet trousers and forcing me down to my knees in front of him. I didn't get to do any work because he began fucking my mouth, holding the back of my head down forcefully, as he forced himself down my throat. I was gagging and tears began rolling down my face but he didn't stop until I threw up, right there all over his dick. He pushed me back on the floor and screamed at me, "Bitch!" As he ran in the bathroom and hopped in the shower, leaving me on the floor to catch my breath.

I was so embarrassed as I gained my composure and peeled myself off the floor. I made my way back up to find my bag so I could clean myself up and brush my teeth. When I made it back to the main pool where everyone was still partying, I grabbed my bag and disappeared again before anyone could stop me. I locked myself in one of the bathrooms and opened my bag to retrieve my toothbrush and mouthwash. After locating it, I looked myself in the mirror and, for a moment, I regretted being there. These men didn't give a fuck about women and it creeped me out but I was in Dubai so I sucked it up and quickly brushed my teeth before gargling with the mouthwash and going back to join the party.

As the day went on, I noticed a lot of the women had begun to be taken away simultaneously. I was seated on the side of the pool with my feet playing in the waterfall when I noticed the guy that I'd puked on speaking to the owner as they stared over at me. I wasn't sure what was going to happen when I saw him begin walking towards me. "You, come with me." The guy demanded, not waiting for me as he turned and began walking. He took me down the long hallway into the last cabin. When I walked in the room there was plastic on the floor like the room back at the mansion and the bed had the same rubber type sheets. "Get undressed, my dad will join you shortly." He said before he exited, closing the door behind him.

I sat on the bed and began to get undressed as I braced myself for a repeat of the previous night. I downed the rest of my drink and placed the cup on the floor next to my bathing suit and laid back on the bed. I sat up when I heard the door open and saw the owner walk into the room with a towel wrapped around his waist. He didn't say anything to me as he climbed on the bed. I remembered he was the one with the smallest penis and came the quickest so I just closed my eyes and waited for him to enter me.

He grunted and told me to open my eyes and "get him back up." so I began licking on his small ass dick and massaging his balls as he moaned and pulled my hair. When he was at full attention, he snatched my head back and directed me to lay back on the bed. To my shock he squatted over me and began grunting as I watched his asshole begin to open up and before I knew it shit was exploding from his ass onto my chest and face. I was completely disgusted as it poured from his bottom onto my body as I tried not to freak out.

When he was done, he stood up and his son entered the room while he walked into the bathroom laughing. I was trying not to get sick to my stomach as I kept reminding myself of all the money, I would get my hands on when this was all over. His son came over and directed me to lay on the plastic covered floor in front of him. When I stood up the shit that had been pooped on me began sliding down my face and chest. I closed my eyes and laid on the floor before he squatted over me and exploded everywhere. The liquified poop seeped into the corner of my mouth and that was it, I was attempting to sit up as I felt the vomit bubbling up my esophagus. This angered him because he turned around and punched me dead in my face. "I'm not done!" He yelled before he screamed something in Arabic. My head was ringing from the blow of his fist but I laid completely still as he finished shitting on my face and chest.

When he was finally done, I was allowed to go into the bathroom and lay on the shower floor where he and his father helped rinse the shit off my face with their piss. I'd never been through something so humiliating and degrading in my life and there was nothing I could do about it at this point. Those men could've killed me for all I knew and there wouldn't be a damn thing anyone could've done about it.

After they were done using me as a human toilet, they both spoke to each other in Arabic and high fived one another before laughing and leaving me there on the floor of the shower. I quickly turned the water to the hottest it would go as I laid on the floor crying to myself as I watched their filth rinse from my body and down the drain.

I stayed in the shower until the water went ice cold but no matter how much soap and water, I used I still smelled them on me. I stepped out of the shower and put my swimsuit back on and made my way back upstairs. When I made it to the deck, I noticed a few of the other girls had returned as well but I felt disgusting. I took a seat at the bar, I wanted to drink until I didn't feel shit, I ordered three shots and a margarita before Mocha came and sat down next to me. "You ok?" She asked me as I stared off at nothing in particular as my mind continued to replay what had just happened. "Not really, you?" Mocha looked just as shellshocked as I did but it was if we both couldn't say he words. I could tell she was holding back tears as she ordered a double shot of Patron before continuing, "Why wouldn't they warn us?" She looked me in the eyes and I could see the tears welling up as the bartender returned with our shots.

I grabbed hers and handed it to her then I picked mine up and downed it. She did the same, wiping her eyes to catch the tears, "I need another one, keep them coming." She said to the woman behind the bar before turning back to me. "I don't think this is worth $70,000 sis I can't lie, I'm ready to go home." I saw she was about to break down and I had to stop her, mostly because I didn't know what these men were capable of, I grabbed her by both of her arms and shook her, "Look we already out here and it already happened. If you leave now you did that shit for 20 racks and THAT definitely ain't worth it. You suck that shit up and cry in your pillow tonight like the rest of us." I said to her as the bartender returned with our next round and my margarita.

We got so drunk at that bar that by the time

the next guy came and got me to take me to the room, which had been cleaned up, I didn't give a fuck. At least this time I knew what to expect when I got naked and laid on the bed before the hairy man told me to turn over as he dropped his towel and entered me slowly from behind. He was stroking me as if I were his long-lost lover as he took slow deep thrusts inside of me as he wrapped his arms around my waist. I was actually beginning to enjoy it as I slowly grinding against him, winding my hips. He began to pick up the pace as he moved his hands to my hips and pulled me back onto him while he continued to thrust inside of me. I could feel myself about to cum as I began to grip his dick with my vaginal walls. He yelled out, "I love you." Before quickly pulling out of me and nutting all over my back. I fell flat on the bed and began to catch my breath before he told me to turn over.

I complied, flipping over to face him. he then got on top of me and took one of the biggest shits I'd ever seen. I was so drunk and exhausted I just laid there with my eyes closed until he was done. When he was done, he went into the bathroom and I just laid there with a million thoughts running through my mind. I heard the door to the room open but I was afraid to open my eyes because of the fecal matter splattered on my face. I felt him climb on the bed a few seconds before I felt him enter my pussy. I never opened my eyes, even when I felt him squat above me and shit all over my face and chest. After the third time I got shitted on it didn't affect me anymore. After six of them did their business on me they all stood and watched as they made me lay on the shower floor before they all peed all over me, laughing and high fiving one another. The entire time they spoke in Arabic so I didn't understand their words but that didn't stop them from taunting me as they laughed at me, making me open my mouth to drink their urine.

After the yacht party, me and the three girls plus the two new ladies, we rode back to the mansion in the limo in silence. I couldn't think of anything but what had just happened. There wasn't enough liquor in the world to help me forget what I'd just gone through. But I refused to cry in front of all those women so I held my composure until I got back to my room. I must've brushed my teeth and gargled 50 times before I scrubbed myself from head to toe in the shower until the water went cold. I got in the jacuzzi tub and soaked for an hour before taking another hot shower and laying in the bed.

I got online and posted a picture in my Versace robe with the caption, "Silk sheets and diamonds, all white." Before logging out and taking my own advice, crying into my pillow.

The next day was New Year's Eve and we all were seated at the dining room table enjoying champagne and endless food as everyone talked as if the day before never happened. I made sure to sit next to Mocha who, surprisingly, was in a good mood as she laughed and joked with the other ladies in attendance. The day was actually going pretty smooth until around 3pm when we were all taken downstairs. The room we entered was already occupied by 10 men, dressed in full sleeved Dishdashis, who were drinking and speaking in Arabic to one another before cheering at our entry. They had us in straight line across the room and demanded that we get undressed.

We all silently removed our clothes and stood there as they examined us and continued speaking in Arabic. For the first time in a long time I was feeling self-conscious as they all examined our bodies, some even sticking their fingers inside of us as they laughed and fondled our breasts. The owner of the house finally walked up and grabbed Strawberry and made her lay down on the floor as he called for his German Shepard dog to come over. I tried to keep a straight face as I witnessed the German Shepard begin licking on Strawberry's vagina. The men all cheered on as he demanded she get on all fours. Y'all, I had never seen no shit like this in my life but I watched as he stood the dog up behind her and forced the German Shepard's penis to enter her.

The dog was humping her hard while she moaned and the men went crazy, throwing money in the air as they danced. I was feeling sick to my stomach but I kept a straight face while the men began grabbing the women from the line to do what they wanted with them. It was like the freak Olympics as two of the men grabbed me and walked me over to a tall chair set up in a corner of the room. Y'all I can't make this shit up, one of the men had a bowl with a live salmon in it and the other was lifting up his Dishdashi and bending over the chair. "Use this." The guy holding the bowl said as he grabbed the wobbling fish and handed it to me. I was so confused but it didn't take

CHAPTER ELEVEN

I always thought my number would be higher but nope, all it took was $70,000 and I'd sold my soul. Even though I was already far from the little girl I was back home, there was no going back after that trip and I knew it. I knew I would never be the same but I did know that my price tag was going up. For the two months after I got back from Dubai, I began smoking a lot more than usual, mostly because I wanted to get high and forget what I'd done, but weed alone wasn't doing it for me. I'd started back snorting coke to numb what I felt every day. To make matters worse my brother's death anniversary passed and I wasn't even allowed to come to his memorial party.

I'd just gotten high with one of the girl's I'd met in Olivia's agency who'd been released from her contract with her. I still didn't know the full story behind what happened but I did know that she stayed on a side of town far away from anyone who knew me or ran in my circle and she had the plug on a good coke connect.

We sat in her living room and got rolled blunts while we talked shit and watched the movie Friday. She stayed off of Camp Creek in Atlanta and anyone who knows Camp Creek they know one side is nice and filled with money, shopping centers, bars, restaurants and $200,000 plus houses; where the other side was filled with dilapidated apartments, liquor stores, gang violence and prostitution. Let's just say her apartment was on the wrong side of the tracks. I didn't mind though because she had the inside laid out and it was a long way from my neck of the woods.

"Bitch what happened with you and ole boy from Africa?" I asked her as I puffed on the blunt in my hand. "Girl that nigga want me to marry him so he can get his papers, but I don't know about that shit." She was lining out a line of coke to snort from her glass coffee table as she sat Indian-style on the floor. "Shit, how much he trying to pay you?" I asked. "See that's not the problem, buddy talking about $20,000 up front and another $5,000 per month for the length of the 3-year contract." She informed me as she snorted a line off the table. "Ok, so what's the problem cause I don't see one." I said with a laugh. It wasn't like she had many options after leaving the agency.

"Girl if we get caught, that is fed time! I'm not trying to go to jail fucking with the government!" She said as I passed the blunt to her. "Bitch please, you know how many people out here doing that shit? Y'all just need to make up ground rules before he gets here, and make that nigga add a new crib in the deal!" I was drinking Hennessey out of the wine glass she'd given me. "Girl you probably right, but I don't play with that jail shit so I'm just a little hesitant. But if he gone get me a crib, we might have to make it do what it do." She said as we shared a laugh and high fived one another.

While we continued talking my phone began to ring and it was Olivia calling to inform me of a in house call request. She said that the clients were celebrities and they wanted to purchase me for the evening. It was already after 3 so I knew I needed to get my ass out of Mercedes' apartment and head home to get prepared for the evening. They were requesting that I accompany them to a night club so after pulling out the perfect fitted Gucci sweater dress and Gucci thigh high boots I jumped in the shower and shaved my legs and trimmed my kitty before bathing and washing my hair.

It took me two and a half hours but I was dressed and ready to walk out the door when the driver text my phone to let me know he was outside. I gave myself one more look over in my wall length full body mirror on my way out the door and I was looking too good not to get a few poses in for the Gram before going downstairs to hop in the all-black SUV waiting for me.

I was driven to a house on the southside in Stockbridge where I was greeted by an older dark skin guy in a tuxedo who welcomed me in and offered to take my fur coat. I looked around at the huge house from the foyer and I was in love with the huge chandelier above me. I followed the older man through the foyer and into the living room of the house where there was loud music blaring through the speakers and the weed smoke was so thick, I caught contact walking through it. I was greeted by the husband-and-wife duo and recognized them immediately as the rapper we will call Leo and his wife, a singer from an old school R&B girl group I grew up on, Mini.

Mini was the first to greet me as she hugged me and complimented me in her thick Atlanta accent. "You wearing the hell out of that dress girl, Moon, right?" She asked. "Yeah, thank you, it's nice to meet you." I responded as she smiled and turned around before calling out, "Aye Larry why don't you fix our guest a drink. You smoke?" She turned back to me and asked. "Not really." I lied. "Well hit this and loosen up, Leo this is Moon, our special guest for the evening." She said to her husband who'd just finished up his conversation with one of the other guys in attendance.

He sipped slowly from his red cup as he looked me up and down. "My my my, what do we have here? Why they call you Moon?" He asked me with a grin. I licked my lips and leaned close to them before answering, "You'd have to bend me over to find out." They both began to laugh as he continued, "Oh yeah I like her!" He threw his arm over my shoulder and the guy Larry walked up and brought me a drink. We all toasted before we continued smoking and talking a bit.

We were only there for about 45 minutes before we hopped in their sprinter to head to the club. When we walked through the Gold Room it was packed wall to wall as the crowd went crazy from our arrival. Leo was very known and loved in the ATL and everyone showed him love in the city. We were escorted to the section and they wasted no time bringing the bottles out. I had my phone out capturing the entire show as the bottle girls twerked and pushed the bottles in the air while the sparklers lit up the dark club.

I sat on the couch and waited for the waitress to hand me a cup while I bobbed to the music. Mini came over and sat next to me and we ended up taking the first shots together. We were getting lit as I danced on her and gave Leo a show. It was if we were the only three people in that club and I was ready to feel Leo inside of me. I wasn't necessarily attracted to Mini but she wasn't bad looking by a long shot. But Leo on the other hand was always sexy to me ever since I was younger. I used to fantasize about what it would be like to be with him and this night was my chance.

We only stayed at the club for a couple hours before Mini grabbed my hand, telling me, "We about to slide." I finished off my drink and followed them back out to the sprinter. "Y'all hungry?" Leo asked as we pulled off from the front of the club. It was me, Leo, Mini and two other girls that rode to the club with us. "Hell yeah, we been drinking like a mufukka too." Mini answered him. "Alright I'm bout to call Larry them and tell them to stop and grab something for all of us from the Waffle House." He pulled out his phone to call his right-hand man as Mini dug into her purse and pulled out an Altoids can, popping it open and taking one out. "Ooh, can I get a mint?" I asked, wanting to get the weed taste out of my mouth. "Oh, baby girl this ain't no mint." She said as she placed it on the tip of her tongue. I realized she was about to pop a molly. I shrugged my shoulders, "Shit I still want one." I said with a laugh. "Come get it." She said, placing another one on the end of her tongue.

I got up from my seat and made my way over to her, bending down to kiss her and suck the molly off of her tongue. Leo ended his phone call and exclaimed, "Oh shit, I knew I liked yo freaky ass, come over here and let me feel some of that tongue action too." He unzipped his pants and pulled his dick out right there. The other two girls began to giggle as one of them got up and came back to where Mini was, lifting her dress and licking on her thighs as I got on my knees in front of Leo.

My jaws were hurting by the time we made it back to their house but I was ready to fuck. Leo's dick wasn't as fat as I would've liked it to be but it was long. Mini was sloppy drunk as we damn near had to carry her upstairs to their bedroom. Leo couldn't wait to get his hands on me as he bent me over the side of their bed and entered me from behind. I was moaning as he stroked me and one of the other girls laid down in front of me and spread her legs. The molly I'd taken had kicked in and I was feeling good as fuck as I ate her pussy. The other girl joined in by sitting on the girl I was going down on face. Mini was so drunk she just laid their playing with herself as she watched.

Leo stopped and pulled out before smacking me on my ass and moving me out the way. "Now you bring yo sexy chocolate ass over here and lick her juices off of daddy dick." He said to the dark skin girl seated on the lighter one's face. She didn't hesitate as she hopped down on the floor and kneeled before him. "Come here." Mini said to me as she got off the bed and walked over to their dresser, pulling out a pair of hand cuffs. She cuffed me to one of the bed posts and made me sit down on the floor while she bent over in front of me and pushed her pussy in my face. I ate her from behind and the brown skin girl got off the bed and kneeled under Leo and began sucking on his balls while the other girl continued giving him head.

The molly we all were on, had us up until 11 am, fucking all over their bedroom and when Leo couldn't get hard anymore, he watched as Mini fucked us with dildos. I passed out from exhaustion and was awakened by the guy Larry who was informing me that a car was waiting for me. I found my phone and realized it was after 5pm and I was still tired, he handed me a bag with an all-star meal from Waffle House in it before walking back out of the room for me to get dressed.

I was all smiles as I checked my bank account and saw the $10,000 that had been transferred that morning from Mini and Leo. I got back to my crib and showered before throwing on my robe and deciding to chill for the day. I plopped down on my couch and scrolled my IG reading comments and DMs when I saw that I had a DM from a rapper that popping and had quite a buzz with one of the top song's on the charts at that time; we will call him Shakeem. I read the DM and it was real simple, he was asking when was the next time I'd be in California and if we could link when I did.

I quickly responded with my phone number before closing out the app and googling his net worth. Shakeem was definitely one of the greats in the making. He was young like me and his rags to riches story was one we all were very familiar with. I was excited as I thought about being the bitch that snagged him early in his career. My phone rang, snapping me out of my thoughts, and I looked down at the screen to see Latasha's face pop up. I rolled my eyes and answered the phone. "Hey, what's up?" I asked, attempting to sound happy to hear from her. "Hey Moon, haven't heard from you I just wanted to check on you and see how things have been. I haven't been able to talk to you for more than four months now. What is going on? Are you mad at me? Did I do something that I don't realize I did? Come on just tell me Princess, cause I feel like I've lost my best friend."

I knew that Latasha probably was one of the most genuine people in my life who'd always had my back but she reminded me too much of how drastically I'd changed over the last three and a half, almost four years. I wanted to break down right then and there and tell my best friend everything. Cry to her and admit to all the crazy shit I'd been doing. All the celebrities I'd met and all the freaky wild sex I was having for money. I wanted to confide in her so badly but that would've made it real. It would've left the door open for judgement and letting her know just how bad I'd been turned out.

That just couldn't happen, so I wiped the single tear from my face before responding, "Girl I have a life I can't be sitting around holding your hand just because you stuck out there with two kids by two different niggas. Please spare me with the sob ass story and why don't we skip right to the end where you ask me for some money and I send it to yo broke ass per usual. How much you need this time Tasha? Which one of the boys need new shoes this month?" I heard her gasp before responding, "Wow, actually you know what me and my boys are good. Don't you worry your pretty little head. I won't ever bother you again." She hung up the phone before I could apologize and tell her I didn't mean what I said. But it was too late, and it needed to be done. I called my girl Mercedes to see if she could pull up with some coke. Of course she was down so I went and grabbed my stash to roll up a few blunts while I waited on her to arrive.

When I opened the door for her, she was dressed in a mini skirt, showing off her long brown legs and the silk knock-off Versace shirt she was wearing had a plunging neck line that showed off her perfectly round, perky breasts. One thing about Olivia, she knew how to spot the baddies and kept nothing but pretty bitches on her roster. Seeing Mercedes walk past me in those stilettos had me wondering what would make Olivia release her from the agency in the first place.

"Hey girl did you eat already?" I asked her as I closed and locked the front door. "Yeah, I'm starving, let's order a pizza or something." She responded as we entered the living room and took a seat on the couch. "Bitch your crib nice as fuck, why you never invited me here before? Yo ass got a view of the whole city from up here!" She complimented me as I turned the TV on. "Girl it's nothing personal, I'm barely here my damn self. Here, find us a good movie or something. You want something to drink?" I asked, tossing her the remote and getting off the couch to head to the kitchen.

I made my way into the kitchen and grabbed a bottle of wine from the fridge before retrieving two wine glasses from the cabinet and going back to join Mercedes in the living room. "You ran up out the crib yesterday quick as fuck, I didn't even get to tell you about Mocha." She said as I took a seat next to her and poured wine into both of our glasses. "Oh shit, what about her?" I asked, handing her one of the glasses before picking up the other and sipping from it. "Girl, a few weeks after y'all came back from Dubai she basically dedicated her life to Christ honey. She is living in some church in Macon on some Nun type shit." She revealed. "I know you fucking lying!" I exclaimed as I sat up on the couch. "If I'm lying, I'm flying. That bitch done changed her whole life around." She said with a laugh.

"You ever been out there to Dubai?" I asked, curious to know how much she knew about the trip. "Nah, I got fired before I ever got booked for Dubai. I heard some crazy shit goes down over there though." She admitted as she finally decided on the movie 'Eve's Bayou', placing the remote back down on the couch before sipping from her glass. "Yeah, some crazy shit did go down, have you talked to Mocha since?" I pried. "Nope, I found out that information from the girl Strawberry at the agency. You know me and her were cool before I got down with Olivia."

"Oh really? I didn't know that; I don't really talk to the girls outside of the meetings and trips. I can't say I'm surprised about Mocha. Anyway," I said, changing the conversation, there was no way I was ready to discuss Dubai with her or anyone for that matter. "You know that nigga Shakeem?" I asked. "Hell yeah, who don't know his fine ass right about now?" She asked as her eyes got big.

"Girl he is fine ain't he? You know anybody that ever dated him?" I wasn't going to tell her that he'd slid in my DM but I did want to see if there was anything crazy, I needed to know about him before I actually met up with him. "He smashed a few chicks I know but they all said he had some good dick and he likes to spend money. Why you asking?"

"Girl no reason, I just been hearing a lot about him that's all." I lied. "But what you waiting on? Let's get the party started." I said. She knew exactly what I meant because she was pulling the coke out of her purse and pouring out some of it onto my coffee table so that we could snort a few lines.

We drank two bottles of wine and snorted 5 or 6 more lines a piece by the time the movie went off. Not that we were really watching it because we were talking about different topics that led to the topic of sex. She shared some of her experiences with me and it made me horny as fuck so I didn't even think twice when she leaned in and kissed me, pushing me back onto the couch as we made out passionately. I stopped her after a few minutes of getting tongued down, "Let's go to my room." I said as we both sat up on the couch.

I led her to the bedroom and lay her down on the bed before having Alexa turn on some slow jams. I watched her slip out of her skirt, exposing her freshly waxed pussy and thick thighs before walking over to the bed to join her. I began softly kissing her lips while I trailed my hand from her knee and up her inner thigh before slipping into her wet opening. I pushed her legs open before I went down and began kissing on her clit. Sweet moans escaped her lips as she squirmed from the sensation. She poured some coke on her stomach and I snorted it before going back down on her.

I really got into it as I licked and sucked on her hardening clit until I felt something wet dripping from my nose. I opened my eyes and saw blood droplets on my sheets from the nose bleed I was experiencing. The next thing I knew I was feeling nauseated so I got out of the bed to make it to the toilet and BAM! I fell straight down on the floor, blacking out before impact.

When I finally opened my eyes, I was laid up in a hospital bed with tubes sticking all out of me. I was scared and confused as I attempted to sit up and realized I had a tube up my nose and down my throat. I quickly pushed the nurse button in a panic and waited until two nurses walked into my room and begin checking the machines I was connected to. "Good morning Ms. Simmons, do you know where you are? Don't speak just shake your head yes or no." One of the nurses asked me as she shined a small light into my eyes. I nodded my head yes as she took my blood pressure. "Do you know what happened to you?" She asked me and I shook my head no.

"The drugs you consumed caused you to go into toxic shock. We are cleaning your blood now and you should be able to go home in 7 to 10 days. The doctor will be in here shortly to explain to you in further detail. If there is anyone you would like me to call to have come down here, write it on the paper next to your bed and I'll come back and get it when I bring your lunch. Try to get you some rest." She said as she adjusted my pillow for me and dimmed the lights.

CHAPTER TWELVE

Even after my brush with death I didn't slow down, in fact, the day I was released from the hospital I went to get a wax and get my hair done in preparation of Shakeem who'd text me and informed me he was coming to Atlanta that night. I'd told him that I was in a bad car accident, of course I didn't tell him the real reason I'd been laid up in the hospital bed when he insisted on facetiming me. But he wanted to see me when I got out and I would be damned if anything would get in the way of that.

I met him at the Waldorf Astoria in his suite and you would've thought we were old lovers who hadn't seen each other in years. He pulled me into the room and wrapped his arms around me, "Damn you smell good, I'm loving this dress." He said as he began to kiss me. I'd bought an orange silk Versace dress specifically for him since he told me it was his favorite color. "I bet it would look better on the floor." He said with a sexy grin as he stepped back and watched me slowly remove the dress, revealing the nude-colored lingerie I was rocking. "Damn you looking good enough to eat! Come over to the window so I can taste you while the city watch."

I turned and seductively looked over my shoulder back at him while he admired my ass bouncing with each step I took. I made it to the patio window and slid the door open before walking out into the cold air, placing both hands on the balcony railing before bending over and giving him a show. He smiled and rubbed his hands together before joining me outside, "Oh, it's like that huh?" I was stepping out of my panties and had placed my hand between my legs to spread my pretty lips for him and he got down and began licking my ass. I continued to play with myself while he bit on my ass while he moaned a bit. I was dripping wet and my body was begging for him to enter me as I began bending over further to guide his tongue to my clit. He was obedient because he stuck his thumb in my butt as he began licking on my clit. I grabbed the railing again with both hands as my eyes rolled in the back of my head from the pleasure.

He ate my pussy for 20 minutes out there on that patio and I came on his face more than 6 times. My legs were weak so he picked me up and took me back inside, tossing me on the bed, before taking his shirt off and hopping on the bed. I was so horny as I begged, "Give me that dick daddy." I began rubbing on his chest and trailed my hand down to pull his dick out of his boxers. He was well endowed to say the least, "Taste it for me first." He was already rock hard so I sat up and put him into my mouth as he sat on his knees above me. "Oooohh shit." He moaned out as I began licking his shaft before spitting on it and taking him whole into my mouth again. "Oh yeah I love that nasty shit." He exclaimed as I really got into it, gargling on him as I pushed him deep in my throat.

He was moaning and curling his toes within 8 minutes of me doing my thing and I guess he couldn't take it anymore because he pulled my head back and told me to turn over and lay on my stomach. I flipped over and laid flat down on the bed and watched as he went and got a condom. After putting it on he grabbed both of my arms and pulled them back towards him as he entered me slowly. He felt so good inside of me as he deep stroked me as if he were making love. I was moaning out and biting my lip as he pulled out and flipped me over, pulling me up on his shoulders and eating my pussy again with me gripping the top of his head. I pulled me back down and guided me onto his dick, holding me close to him, he laid his head on my chest as I slowly rocked my swirled my hips in a circular motion slowly.

I don't know what it was but it felt like we were legit making love. He was so delicate with me and attentive to my body while focused on pleasing me before pleasing himself. I can't lie while we were fucking, I was thinking that there was a possibility that this could be my soul mate. I fell asleep in his arms that night and when I woke up the next morning, he'd ordered room service for breakfast, we sat down and ate together. He was pretty cool and a lot more romantic than he portrayed himself in his songs. We had a lot in common as far as our upbringing but he was a couple years older than me.

"What are your plans for the rest of the week?" He asked me as he simultaneously went through the three phones he had in front of him on the table. "Nothing really, you know I'm technically supposed to be resting from this car accident." I said as I took pictures of my food before digging into the French toast on my plate. "Shit you definitely wasn't doing no resting last night." He said with a laugh. I couldn't help but giggle, "Shut up, that was all you. I was trying to mind my business."

"I'm trying to mind yo business in Puerto Rico if you down." My eyes lit up, "For real?" I asked. "Yeah, for real. I'm feeling you and I got a lil vacation time, the jet leaves in a few hours so you can go home and grab some stuff to wear, orrrr...." He paused. "Or what?" I asked, intrigued. "Or we can finish breakfast, take a shower, fuck a few more times and go shopping when we get out there." He said as he got up from the other side of the table, passionately kissing me as he choked me slightly. "Well, I like whatever option gets me those lips on these right here right now on top of all this food." I said jokingly. I guess Shakeem was bout that life because he picked me up and placed my naked body on top of the table full of food. I could feel the sticky syrup on my back as he opened my legs and grabbed one of the fresh strawberries on the table and placed it in his mouth. He began eating me out, smashing the strawberry juices inside me as he pleased me. This nigga was trying to make a bitch fall in love!

Our trip to Puerto Rico was lit but we both decided not to post anything to our social media until we returned. I was used to that with most of the celebrities I'd dated so it was cool with me. We stayed out there for 6 days and when I tell you we fucked in so many positions and rooms in that villa it was crazy. When I got back home, I was on cloud 9 as I lay across my bed thinking back to my crazy week with Shakeem. My phone had been on DND since I was released from the hospital and I wasn't ready to come down from the natural high I was feeling. The craziest and most confusing part to me was, I was feeling like this and hadn't made one dime off the nigga.

I went to his IG page to see if he'd posted anything yet but he hadn't. I decided to hold off as well, I wasn't trying to have the blogs in our business anyway. I got bored and ended up checking my email and I had at least 25 messages from Olivia so I decided to give her a call, knowing I'd missed out on some money. "Hello?" Olivia answered the phone. "Hey girl, I'm sorry I been MIA. So much shit been going on the last couple weeks." I explained. "Moon what is my number one rule in this shit?" She asked me in a serious tone. "Huh? What you mean?" I was genuinely confused. "Moon when I brought you on, I told you that the rules were no freelance dating or fucking anyone that didn't go through me. So, you can imagine my disappointment when

I found out you were laid up in the Waldorf with Shakeem!" I was busted. There was nothing for me to say so I just listened.

"I really liked you that's the crazy part but I have to let you go." I can't lie I didn't see that coming but I'd learned a long time ago to never beg anyone for anything no matter the circumstance. "I understand. I apologize for not telling you, and." Olivia had ended the call before I could finish my sentence. To be honest, I hadn't even thought about her or the agency when Shakeem hit me up, I was just enjoying being treated like a person and not a business transaction. I felt like maybe it was time for me to walk away, I had well over $400,000 in the bank and it seemed like dating was a true possibility for me. I looked at it as a blessing in disguise, a fresh start.

The next day I decided to get some retail therapy and took myself to Buckhead to shop. I was walking through the mall when I was approached by a tall dark skin brother with smooth chocolate skin, nice white teeth, a low cut rippled with waves and broad shoulders. "Excuse me beautiful, could I get a moment of your time?" He asked in his African accent. "Depends on what you want." I said as I leaned back, holding my bags. "I would love to maybe take you to dinner tonight or something, that is if you don't have any other plans, I'm Jafari, nice to meet you." He said as he held out his hand for mine. I placed my hand in the palm of his and he kissed the back of it. "I'm Moon, and I think that we could make that happen." I smiled. "Cool, take my number down and call me when you leave the mall."

I shopped for a few hours until I ran out of stores I liked before buying a pretzel and heading back home. My phone began to ring when I hopped on the highway and it was a California area code. "Hello?" I answered as I maneuvered through traffic. "Hey beautiful, I'm in yo city and I'm trying to see you." I recognized Titan's voice immediately, the LA basketball player I'd fucked after Chanel's house warming party. After that weekend together he'd call me every time he was in town but I hadn't really talked to him in a month or so. "You changed your number again I see." I stated. "Yeah, you know I gotta keep em guessing." He said with a laugh, "But I got a spot out here in Alpharetta, you pulling up on me right?"

"Yeah, send me the address and I'll pull up on you later." After catching up for a few minutes I ended the call as I got off my exit. Pulling up to my house I was surprised to see a black Range Rover parked in the parking deck, in my spot. I got out of my car and walked up to the tinted window, knocking on it. "Hey, who are you looking for?" I asked, unable to see inside. The door to the truck opened and it was Shakeem. "Hey, what are you doing here? How you know where I live?" I asked as I gave him a hug. "I have my ways, and I had to get some of that one more time before I hit the road." He said as he leaned down and kissed me. I giggled as he grabbed my hand and lead me to the front door.

"You popping up and shit like we go togetha or somethin'"I said jokingly as we walked inside my crib. "Shit, you keep putting it on a nigga like you did last night and I'm most definitely gonna have to cuff you, where your bathroom at?" He asked as I sat my keys on the counter and took my jacket off. I heard my phone buzz and looked down to see Titus' name at the top of the screen, texting me his location. I quickly turned my phone on DND before going into my bedroom to get undressed.

Shakeem came out of the bathroom and made his way over to where I was seated at the foot of the bed, naked. "Oh, you ready for me too huh?" He asked as he unzipped his pants and pulled out his hardening penis. "I'm ready to taste daddy dick." I said as I grabbed it and began licking the tip. He moaned as I opened my mouth and placed it inside as I swirled my tongue around, driving him crazy as he looked down at me and began squeezing on my breasts. I pulled him deeper into my throat as I stared up in his eyes. He was exploding in my mouth seconds later. "Whooo shit! You got a nigga knees weak and shit." He laughed as he fell back on the bed to regain his composure. "You nasty as fuck, come here let me get some of that tight ass pussy." He said before I wrapped both of my legs around his waist and rode him until he was busting inside of me, kissing my neck and professing his love to me as he released.

Shakeem did not want to leave and I knew I needed to get ready to go see Titus so I was relieved when after I offered to order us some food, he realized he had a flight to catch in just two hours. He kissed me good-bye and promised to call when he landed in Toronto. After walking him outside I locked my door before running a hot bath and grabbing one of my Douches from under the bathroom cabinet. I got in the tub and squirted the contents inside of my throbbing pussy before sitting in the tub to soak.

After showering and getting dressed I was pulling up to the house Titus was staying in for the weekend. I buzzed the gate and waited a bit for the gates to open and drove up the winding driveway to the huge house on a hill. I parked right in front of the home and got out, walking up the huge stone stairs in my knee-high Louboutin black boots. The trench coat I was wearing protected me from the cruel March winds since the Prada dress I was wearing barely covered my most private parts. I rang the doorbell and Titus opened the door with his shirt off. "Damn, you looking good, where you coming from?" He asked me as I walked inside and removed my coat. "From my house." I responded with a laugh as I looked around the huge home. "Oh, so this all for me?" He asked with a sexy grin. "Yeah, all for you." I said before kissing him on the lips. "Don't start no shit now, I'll bend you over this mufukkin ottoman right here right now fuck you mean?" He said, smacking me on the ass with a laugh.

"Nah but a few of the guys are here with their girls, come on so I can get you a drink." He grabbed my hand and lead the way, asking me about my day and shit like that while we were walking. Y'all when we bent that corner to enter the living room, I wanted to shit a brick. Right there, laughing it up as they played spades, was the basketball player I'd jacked off on the Wayne's yacht out in California. "What you want to drink? We got everything up in this bitch." He asked me as I tried to act as normal as possible. I mean the shit happened over 8 months prior and he was a professional athlete so there was no way he would've remembered me, right?

After making me a drink he asked me to follow him over to the spades table because he had next. I didn't know what to do as we made our way over to the table the four guys were seated at. There were several other people around the room while music played and everyone drank. My heart had to be racing a mile a minute as I kept sipping from my cup and looking down at my phone. "Hey, you good?" Titus asked, looking down at me. "Yeah, just wasn't expecting a party that's all." I was literally in no mood to be around all those people. Honestly, I was ok with going to his room and scrolling my social media while I drank my Henny. "You trying to go to my room or something?" He asked me, wrapping his arm around my neck. "Do you mind?" I asked, looking up into his eyes. "Nah I don't mind, aye y'all I'll be back later, hold it down." He said as he led me away from the small crowd and up the stairs to the master bedroom.

He closed the door as I looked around the spacious room. "So, you got me all to yourself, what you gone do with me?" he asked as he walked up behind me, wrapping his arms around my waist as he began kissing on my neck. "What you want me to do to you big daddy?" I asked as I rubbed my ass against his hardening dick. "Come show me that lil thing you do with your tongue." He said, backing up and smacking me on the ass. "Go lay on the bed." He instructed me. "Lay down this way with your head off the side." He said as he took his pants off. I did as I was told before this nigga had me giving head upside down. My head was hanging off the side of the bed while he fucked my mouth and in some strange way, I liked it. I massaged his balls while he thrust himself into my throat.

He pulled back and picked me up as I wrapped my legs around his waist, he guided me onto his rock-hard penis. He carried me over to the wall and placed my back up on the wall before deep stroking me as I bit on his ear and scratched as his head, moaning is pleasure as his curved dick hit my G-spot. After I had an orgasm, he flipped me over the side of the bed, placing one of his legs on the base of the headboard before entering me from behind. I screamed out in ecstasy as he dove deep inside me with slow steady thrusts. "Whose pussy is this?" He asked me, smacking me on the ass before picking up his pace. "Yours." I moaned. "Whose pussy is this? What you say?" He took his leg down from the bed and pushed my ass up and began eating my pussy. "Oooohh shit. This your pussy big daddy." I moaned out in pleasure.

He flipped me back over and entered me again from behind, pulling my hair and smacking my ass as he gave me deep penetration. "Cum on daddy dick right now." He demanded in a sexy tone. I closed my eyes and concentrated on the nut and not even one minute later I was squirting onto his dick while he was busting his load inside of me. Man, that shit felt so good as I felt his dick throbbing inside of me as he caught his breath before pulling out. "Girl you got some good ass pussy; I can't even lie." He said as he laid on the bed next to me. I just laughed as I made my ass jiggle, laying on my belly. "Look at yo freaky ass, you ready for round two already ain't you?" He asked with a laugh, rolling on his side and biting me on my ass.

CHAPTER THIRTEEN

Shakeem had just came again and rolled over to answer his ringing phone, "Talk to me." He answered before he paused briefly, "Yeah, give me 30 minutes I'll be at the studio in Marrietta." He ended the call and turned his attention to me as I caught me breath, lying naked on top of his sheets. "You gone be here when I get back?" He asked me as he got out of the bed. "Keem, I been here for two weeks already, I do have a crib I have to take care of as well." I laughed as I sat up on the bed. "Yeah, but we could change that if you'd stop playing with a nigga." He said, staring at me as I sat up on the bed. "Baby you know you got a lot going on and we only been talking for two months." I mean don't get me wrong, Shakeem was literally a woman's dream, financially, physically, sexually and all but I was so afraid of getting deep with him and my past coming back out to bite me in the ass that I was pushing him away.

"Baby, a real man doesn't need a lifetime to know when he's found the one." He leaned down and kissed me before walking into his bathroom. I grabbed my phone off his nightstand and took a picture of the new iced out Rolex Shakeem had just given me on my wrist, before posting it with the caption, "I got time today." Being sure to get his silk Versace sheets in the picture. After looking through all of my social media pages I grabbed the remote and turned on one of the 3 mounted TVs in his room.

I waited until Shakeem left to roll out of bed and get ready for the day. It was the end of May so I was preparing for my 22nd birthday party and I had a lot to do. After getting dressed I hopped in the early birthday present from Shakeem and headed to the party planner's office. Shakeem had purchased me an all red 2018 Mercedes-Benz GLE! I was pleased with the event planner who assured me that everything was right on schedule and she'd be able to execute my wishes of a casino night theme. I'd booked with -The Biltmore Ballroom and Shakeem had used some of his connects to get me the best casino equipment, tables, and even 20 slot machines! After leaving the party planner's office I headed to my appointment with the designer that was creating my extravagant birthday gown.

I was standing on the raised pedestal as the seamstress, India, got my last measurements. Girl either you've gained a little weight since our last fitting or you're bloated like crazy." She informed me as she showed me her previous markings. I had been eating a little more than usual but it was because I was always smoking with Shakeem and we'd eat up any and everything we wanted afterwards. I knew with only a week left until the party I had no time to try to diet so she was stuck with my cupcake stage body.

"Girl that's that good loving weight." I said with a laugh as she finished up. "Well, this week I'm gone need you to be eating less and drinking more water. The dress is made to be extremely tight around your midsection, you don't want a lil pudge throwing off your look." She added. "You right! I'm wearing my waist trainer and drinking my tea all week!" I said as I tried to suck my stomach in as I looked in the dull length mirror in front of me. "Alright, the party is next Saturday so I'll come to you Thursday with the dress that way if there are any further alterations, I can get them done in time, sound good?" She asked as she grabbed my hand and helped me down. "Sounds good, I'll see you then. Thank you again."

I walked out of the boutique as my phone began to ring, "Hello?" I answered, getting into my truck. "Hey sexy, I'm in yo city but just till the morning, can I see you?" Titus asked through the receiver. I can't even lie; Titus had some good dick. That's why it was so hard for me to tell him no any time he hit my line. "You know it's all about you, send me your location I can pull up on you now since I know you gonna need your rest for that game tomorrow night."

"Aight bet, I'll see you in a minute. Have you eaten?" He asked me as I hopped on the highway. "Nah, not yet."

"Cool, I'll order us something, I'm staying at The St. Regis hotel, I'll text you my room number." We ended our call and I headed towards his hotel. When I arrived, he let me in the room and gave me a kiss on the lips before smacking me on my ass. "Where you was coming from?" He asked me. "Why? I look good don't I?" I laughed, placing my hands on my hips. "You always look good, but you getting thick as fuck on me ain't ya?" He walked up to me and wrapped his arms around my waist and kissed me again, grabbing two handfuls of my ass as we locked lips.

"Ok so you the second person that told me that today! Before I came here, I had a fitting with the designer making my birthday dress and she said I gained weight since the last fitting just one month ago." I shook my head. "Shit yo ass better not be pregnant." He said, kissing me on the forehead as we heard the concierge knocking on the door bringing the food he'd ordered. "Hey baby I gotta go to the bathroom real quick." I excused myself and ran in the bathroom. I tried to remember the last time I'd had my period and for the life of me I couldn't remember. It had to have been at least two months since I'd bought tampons. I began freaking out as I looked at myself in the mirror. "Fuck!" I whispered as I began to realize my ass was definitely pregnant.

I walked back out of the bathroom after regaining my composure and Titus was going through the bags of Chinese food. "You aight? I got you the beef and broccoli with shrimp fried rice." He told me as I walked up to the table, he was separating the food on. "Yeah, I'm good, I know I'm starvin like Marvin though, let me get that." I laughed, grabbing my plate out of his hand. We both sat at the table and ate our food as we caught up with one another. "Can you believe we've known each other for a year now?" I asked him as I sat back in the chair looking over at him. I didn't want to accept it but I knew that I was pregnant by either Titus or Shakeem, but I didn't want to ever have to admit it to either of them. They were taking very good care of me and I wasn't trying to ruin that by getting pregnant and having to explain how I wasn't sure who the father was.

"Damn that's right cause you were just about to turn 21 then. That's crazy, time flies when you having fun." He said with a laugh as he stood up and walked over to me, bending over to kiss me while he stuck one of his hands up my skirt and the other through my hair as he sucked on my tongue. "Open your legs." He said to me before taking off his shirt and getting on the floor in front of me. He lifted my skirt and stuck his head under as I parted my legs for him. He began flicking his tongue over my clit while I moaned out in pleasure. He slid two of his fingers in and out of me slowly as he licked and sucked on my clit. It didn't take long for my body to respond, squirting into his mouth as I moaned loudly, "I wanna feel you daddy, give it to me, give me that big ass dick I been missing." I pleaded, staring down at him.

He stood to his feet and had me bend over the back of the chair before he pushed all of himself into my warm, dripping opening. I started doing my Kegels on him as he stroked deep inside of me. "Shit, you feel good as fuck." He moaned as he picked up the pace. He began diving deeper and deeper inside of me as he pulled back on my hair and stuck one of his thumbs inside my ass. I was screaming out in ecstasy as he released his seed inside me while I came on his dick.

We fucked a few more times before I went home to shower and douche because I knew Shakeem was going to want me back at his crib for the night. After getting myself dressed and smelling good I called Shakeem's phone, "Hey sexy what you got going on?" He asked me as he answered the phone. I could hear music in the background so I knew he was still at the studio. "Nothing just left a late lunch with my homegirl, was trying to see if I should head home or come to you, but I see you still out handling your business so you can hit me up when you finish." I lied. "Oh, nah baby you can come to the studio, can you grab me some more backwoods on your way?"

I pulled up the studio and it was the typical scene, with a thick cloud of weed smoke, random groupies and a bunch of his entourage drinking and listening to the magic Shakeem and his engineer was creating. "Hey sexy, you grab the woods?" He greeted me, kissing me on the lips. "Yeah, here you, I'm not interrupting anything am I?" I asked as I handed him the backwoods pack from my purse, not that I gave a fuck for real. "Hell nah, matter of fact I want you to hear this new track I'm working on. Aye y'all can gone ahead and head to the club, me and my lady about to rock out for the remainder of the session." He said, cutting the music and excusing the room.

Everyone said their good byes as they grabbed their belongings and cleared the studio. "What? You clearing rooms for little ole me?" I asked as I took a seat in one of the cushioned rolling chairs. "Baby it's all about you, now let me introduce you to my world." He said, taking a seat in the chair next to mine as he began turning up the music and starting the track over. He and I bobbed our heads as it played before he cut it down again. "I feel like it's missing something, I just can't put my finger on it." He said, turning his attention over to me. "Yeah, like it should have a harder bass drop before the hook and maybe speed up the flow." I suggested, I didn't know much about making music, but Latasha and I used to be a girl rap group when we were in school and I did know what got the clubs moving. He smiled at me before saying, "Let me find out you know a little somethin somethin. How was your day? I see you looking good as fuck, where y'all go eat at?" He asked me, pulling my chair closer to him as we faced each other.

I had to think quick and just blurted out the first place I could think of, "Ruth Chris over there off of Roswell road. But thank you baby, you been up here all day have you even eaten?" I asked, quickly changing the subject. "Yeah, one of the guys ordered us some pizza and shit earlier, but I ain't gone lie a nigga need some dessert right about now." He smiled, pushing my knees apart and trailing one of his fingers up my thigh and underneath the brown and red Dior dress I was rocking. His eyes lit up when he realized I wasn't wearing any panties and he wasted no time tasting my juices and fucking me all over that studio.

CHAPTER FOURTEEN

"Congratulations Ms. Simmons you are expecting and your projected due date is going to be." The doctor said, looking down at my chart before continuing, "December 18th 2018, you'll need to fill this prenatal vitamin prescription as well as the pills for your low iron." I couldn't believe it but I had already known. I put off going to the doctor until after my birthday party because I wanted to be able to get fucked up with a clear conscious. But there I was finding out that I was pregnant and I didn't know which of these niggas was the daddy. I remember thinking to myself that there was no need on that doctor wasting his time writing that prescription because there was no way I was keeping that mufukka.

I left the doctor's office with my paperwork and "baby's first picture" and headed straight to the crib to look up some abortion clinics. I pulled into the parking deck and hopped out my truck, paperwork in hand, and made my way into the building. I walked into my crib and to my surprise it was filled with balloons and red roses everywhere. "Happy birttthhdayyy tooo yoouuuuuu." I heard the beautifully familiar voice of the one and only, I'll call her Kelly Cash, as she stood next to Shakeem in my living room. "Oh my god!" I exclaimed as I listened to her sing to me. Shakeem had been away on the road on my birthday and this was his way of surprising me and making up for it. He walked over to me and grabbed all my belongings out of my hands and turned to put everything on the counter top when the sonogram picture fell out onto the floor. Shakeem squinted his eyes and bent down to pick the picture up. "What is this?" He asked, looking back at me.

Kelly finished my birthday song as things got kind of awkward, Shakeem was staring at me then back at the sonogram, then back at me. I couldn't read his face to know if he was happy or not so I just stayed silent and began smiling to see what his reaction would be. "Imma be a daddy?" He asked excitedly. Shakeem didn't have any kids and, what I didn't know was, he wanted so badly to be a father. I shook my head yes as he scooped me up in his arms, "Are you serious? Oh my god! I love you girl." He said before kissing me. He'd never said those three words to me before and that shit turned me on. I didn't see Kelly leave but I'm sure she didn't stay much longer because he took me into my bedroom and made love to me.

I didn't know what to do, I didn't expect for Shakeem to find out I was pregnant and since he'd found there was no way he would agree with me getting an abortion. The weeks following him discovering the sonogram picture he was spoiling the shit out of me. He'd already begun converting one of his bedrooms in his Atlanta house into a nursery and started discussing me moving in with him. Shakeem had no idea that Titus was shooting the club up right along with his ass. I knew that if he ever found out it would be the end for us.

I didn't know what to do but my mind hadn't changed, there was absolutely no way I was having that child. I decided to pull up on Mercedes at her crib to talk. I really didn't have many girlfriends so Mercedes and I had been getting close by default. When I got to her crib, we smoked some weed as we caught up with one another. Mercedes had taken the African up on his offer and was waiting for him to make the transition to the states to marry her. When she found out I was pregnant and wanted an abortion the first thing out her mouth was, "Bitch you bout to be set for life! Fuck you mean you don't wanna keep the baby?"

"Bitch I'm only 22, I'm still living my life. I don't want no damn baby fucking up my body! But it don't matter cause if I get an abortion, he'd never forgive me." I admitted as I shook my head. "Well even though I think you making a bad decision I understand where you coming from. I mean I know an herb you can drink that could force a miscarriage but that shit may or may not work and it's gone be painful as fuck either way." Mercedes said as she puffed from the blunt in rotation. "Nah, I need something more certain, especially if it's gonna be painful." I admitted. "Well shit I could get some of the niggas from around the way to beat yo ass, get that baby right on up out of you." She said with a laugh, passing the blunt.

I wasn't laughing, I was considering what she said. "You know somebody for real?" I asked her with a straight face. She burst out laughing but I didn't flinch. "Oh, you dead ass?" She asked, confused. "Bitch I need a baby like I need a fucking hole in my head. If you know a nigga that'll fake rob me and beat me up, I'll pay that nigga and everything. That shit just can't be traced back to me so when you set that shit up, I need you to make it seem like you hiring the nigga to beat my ass, not that I'm doing it you know?" I asked her as I chiefed on the blunt. "Girl yo ass crazy as hell, but I got you. Let me know when you trying to make this shit happen and I'll set it up."

Two weeks later I was getting out of my truck to head into my apartment when I saw two men jump from behind one of the parked cars and begin to chase me. I tried to get into the building but couldn't get my key pass out fast enough before one of the two masked men grabbed me by the hair and snatched me behind one of the cars, away from the cameras that captured my performance. He pinned me on the ground as the shorter of the two guys began stomping and kicking me hard in the stomach. "Not my face." I whispered as they both began wailing on me before taking my purse and running out of the parking garage where Mercedes was waiting for them in a parked car.

I lay there in the parking garage screaming for help as I called 911 from my cell phone. I felt wetness between my legs and when I looked down, I could see blood pooling in the middle of my legs, staining my jeans. I cried out as I waited for help to arrive. It seems like it took forever for an ambulance to show up but I passed out from blood loss before they closed the doors to the back of it. I was rushed to the hospital where I found out I was successful in terminating my four-and-a-half-month pregnancy.

I called Shakeem, sounding as sad as possible, forcing myself to cry I told him, "Baby some guys jumped me in the parking garage at my house and they beat me real bad." I burst into tears as I tried to act distraught. "Moon, calm down, where are you?" Shakeem asked sounding concerned. "I'm down at Emory." I sobbed. "I'm on my way right now baby, I'm on my way to you right now you hear me?" He assured me before ending the call.

Forty five minutes later Shakeem was entering my hospital room with worry filled eyes as his body guards stood outside my hospital room. "Baby, what the fuck happened?" He rubbed my head and belly as he spoke. I closed my eyes before taking a deep breath to inform him, "The baby didn't survive the attack. They killed our baby!" I screamed out, burying my head in the palm of my hands to conceal the fact that no tears were coming from my eyes as I sobbed. Shakeem was silent as he kneeled down on one knee as if the wind had left his body. "I'm so sorry baby." He said soothingly as he held my hand and lay his head on my leg. I could feel his tears as they splashed against my skin and I honestly felt bad for him. I knew he genuinely loved me but I was so fucked up in the head I thought in some twisted way I was protecting him.

CHAPTER FIFTEEN

After I was released from the hospital Shakeem refused to let me go back to my apartment. I stayed with him for the 8 weeks the doctors gave me to recover and then he handed me the keys to my own condo, paid in full and in my name. We'd only been dating for six months but Shakeem was head over heels in love with me. "Where we going?" I asked in anticipation from the passenger seat of Shakeem's G-Wagon, blindfolded. "Just chill baby, we almost there." He assured me as the truck slowed down before coming to a stop. He walked over to my side, opened my door, and helped me out. "Okay so I know you been kind of down and out since we lost our baby girl four months ago so I wanted to do something to cheer you up." He said as he removed my blindfold.

When I opened my eyes, I had to blink a few times to make sure I wasn't seeing things. The moniker on the front window spelled out, MOON'S SALON AND SPA, in big bold red letters. "Oh my god! No you didn't!" I said as I covered my mouth in shock. "Anything for you." He said as he pulled out the keys and handed them to me. I jumped up and down before kissing him and wrapping my arms around his neck to hug him tight as I thanked him. "Come on, I wanna show you inside." He said, taking my hand and allowing me to unlock the glass doors.

"Now it's not all the way done yet because I knew you would want to decorate and furnish it yourself but see this would be your lobby or waiting area. You could put a casing up here and sale hair products or some shit. Then if you walk with me over here, you'll see that the square footage gives you enough space to fit at least 12 booths comfortably. Behind here is a private suite that you can use your imagination with, back here would be the shampoo area and there are two bathrooms down there." I followed beside him as I took it all in, being sure to snap pictures and videos for my social media. I could picture it all coming together. I didn't know anyone in the damn hair business but I figured it was Atlanta so I'd find stylist with a little promotion. Thankfully I'd done at least one thing right in going to cosmetology school and getting my license.

"I absolutely love this place! I can't believe you did this for me." I said as I looked around still in shock. "Wait till you see what's up here." He smiled as he led me up the stairs inside the shop.

"Oh my god! I fucking love you!" I yelled as I saw the fish tank that was built into one the walls. "I know you always said you liked fish tanks so I got you one. You can pick the fish you want to put in there. Over here will be the massage area." Shakeem went on describing his vision for the spa area but I found him so attractive in that moment all I could think about was him fucking me right there against that empty fish tank. I dropped my coat and pulled my sweater dress over my head as he continued. He turned back to face me and his eyes lit up seeing me standing there in my boots and bra, since I wasn't wearing panties.

"Ok then!" He said with a laugh, "Bring that sexy ass here then." He said as I walked over to him and unzipped his pants while I stuck my tongue down his throat. I allowed his pants to hit the ground as I used them for a little cushion for my knees on the wooden floors. I took him into my mouth and slurped loudly as he leaned back against the tank.

After we left my new salon, for just a split second, I felt bad because out of all the people I wanted to share the good news with I wasn't on good terms with any of them. The part that was really setting in was that Thanksgiving was two weeks away and Shakeem was asking that my family join us in his hometown of Ohio. I had been lying to him about our relationship status but the closer we were coming to the holidays the more pressure I felt.

Shakeem was on the road a lot and this day was no different. After he dropped me off at home to get ready for his flight, I decided to try to give one of my brothers phones. I called Marvin first and he answered on the first ring. "Hello?"

"Hey Marv! How's it going?" I asked nervously. "What's up Moon, you aight?" He asked dryly. "Yeah, I'm good I just wanted to call and check on you." I said as I sat on my couch. "Oh word? That's what's up, you taking care of yourself out there?" He asked. "Yeah, I'm doing ok for myself, working on some things to get me out of the shop I'm working at. How has everyone been? How's mom and dad?"

"Everybody good, maybe you should call them and check on them too. It's been way too long." I mean I felt him but my dad had made it very clear nine months prior that he was done with me. He did that by banning me from MJ's memorial party. "Yeah, I know Marv, but daddy don't wanna hear from me." I admitted as I dropped my head. "When was the last time you tried?" Marvin's voice made me miss home I can't lie. Being around Shakeem, who was very family oriented, forced me to have to relive my childhood memories when we'd have our deep conversations.

"When he told me I wasn't welcome to MJ's memorial back in February."

"I don't know sis, reach out to him and if that don't work call mom, I know she misses you and would love to hear from you." He told me before his line beeped, "Hey Moon I gotta take this, it was really nice hearing from you. I love you kid."

"I love you too bro." I said as I wiped a single tear from my face as it slid down my cheek. I ended the call and scrolled down to my mother's number and held my breath as I hit call. She didn't answer the phone, I knew it was because she didn't recognize the number but I still was disappointed. I wasn't ready to face my dad so I got up off the couch and went to take a bubble bath.

I was relaxed and sipping my wine while I sat in the hot water and reminisced. my thoughts were interrupted by my ringing cell phone and looking at the caller ID I saw it was my mother returning my call. "Hello?" I answered nervously. "Princess? Is that you?" She asked, anxiety filling her voice. "Yeah, it's me ma, how are you?" I asked as I sat up in the tub. "I'm so glad you called baby, is everything okay?" She asked as her anxiety turned to worry. "Yeah, everything is fine ma, I just miss you that's all." I admitted as the tears poured from my eyes. "Hmmm, does that mean you will be at your grandmother's house for Thanksgiving dinner this year?"

"Well see that's the thing, my boyfriend wanted you guys to come to Ohio for the holiday, he's gonna put y'all in first class and everything! You, dad and the boys." I said, trying to sound extra excited. My mom got silent and for a moment and I broke it by asking, "Ma? You heard me?"

"Yeah, I heard you. I can't believe you said it, but I heard you." She said disappointed. "Princess you haven't been home in almost 2 years and you want us to up and fly out to some stranger's house for Thanksgiving?" She laughed. "You really have some nerve. Look, if you want to see your family for the holidays then you need to be on a first-class flight out here and if your lil boyfriend want to meet us then he can accompany you here Princess." My mom was adamant about what she was saying. I promised her that I'd try my best to make it before telling her I loved her and ending the call to answer my other line.

It took some convincing but I eventually got Shakeem to agree to come to St. Louis with me for Thanksgiving if I promised to come to Ohio for Christmas. So, two weeks later we were checking into our suite at the Four Seasons in St. Louis. Shakeem literally had to work up until the day before Thanksgiving so by the time we got there it was late night so we decided to grab something to eat and retire to the room for the rest of the night.

The next day was Thanksgiving and I got dressed in the olive-green Gucci turtle neck dress and burgundy ankle boots Shakeem bought me to match his burgundy tailored Gucci suit. He had an olive-green fedora on that matched his Gucci loafers. We looked damn good as we posed and took pictures together in the mirror on my phone. "Why you be taking all these pictures of us but never post them? Yo ass post everything but me." Shakeem said with a laugh as he stood behind me with his hands wrapped around my waist as we stood in the mirror. "Baby the moment we post each other is the moment our relationship is no longer our relationship. I'm not ready to let the outside in just yet." I said, looking back at him and kissing his lips.

"So, you saying you ready to be in a relationship with me?" He asked with a smile, squeezing my hips. "Keem, you about to meet my parents and they haven't met anyone since my high school boyfriend. That should tell you something." I assured him. I hated to admit it but I was falling in love with Shakeem. I was finally beginning to let my walls down and let him in. "Yeah, it tells me that you need to post one of them mf pictures because I just posted and tagged you on my story." He said, showing me his phone. "Oh my god Keem you play all day!" That was it, we were official.

We arrived at my grandmother's house with four bottles of liquor and a few bottles of wine. My family didn't drink often but they all got wasted on holidays so I made sure that we stopped at the liquor store and grabbed something for everyone. "Heeeyyyy granny!" I exclaimed when I walked in the front door. My grandmother, at 83 years old, was a beautiful black woman with thick black hair she kept braided in two corn rows. She was very petite and was indeed the backbone of the

Simmons's family.

She looked up from the stove, looking over the top of her glasses, "Is that my Princess?" She was holding her chest in shock when she realized her eyes were not deceiving her. My grandmother hadn't seen me in four years and I missed her cooking. Being inside her house had a flood of emotions flowing through me as she embraced me. "Oh, my goodness, look at you, you are beautiful! Who is this fine gentleman you done brought with you?" My grandma asked as Shakeem placed the liquor on the table. "I'm Shakeem, nice to meet you. You throwing down in here I see, would you like me to pop one of these bottles and make you a glass of wine?" Shakeem offered, holding up two of the wine bottles.

My grandmother turned to me and smiled, "Oh, I like you already, I'll take the red one. Moon, make sure you go back there and speak to your cousins they out in the backyard, I know they gonna just go crazy when they see you. You know they think you a celebrity or something." She said with a laugh as she walked back over to the stove to stir the greens. "Ok, Keem you coming with me or you staying in here?" I asked as he poured my granny her wine. "One second, I'll come with you."

We made our way through my grandmother's house and out the sliding back door. My cousins were outside playing flag football with my brothers and the younger ones were engaged in an intense Nerf war. "What up y'all!" I exclaimed, walking outside. "Oh my god It's Moon!" One of my little cousins, Meka, screamed before she took off running towards me. Before I knew it, I had 16 arms around me giving me hugs and bombarding me with questions, until they realized who Shakeem was. They lost their minds! I loved how Shakeem posed for pictures with all my little cousins for their social media and even though he didn't play the flag football, he did take my cousins up on their challenge at Madden on the PS3.

It felt good sitting back and being around the family but when my parents arrived my father still didn't have many words for me. "Alright y'all, we all about to get washed up and say grace so we can dig in." My grandmother announced as I made my third Hennessey and Coke. The doorbell rang and I made my way to the front to answer while my brothers helped my mom set the table and my older cousins helped the younger ones wash their hands. When I opened the door, my face dropped when I saw Latasha and the boys. "Oh, I didn't know you were coming this year." She said as she twisted her face.

Latasha and I had been friends so long that it was normal for her to come to my family events with or without me. My parents treated her like another child and so my family treated her as such so I wasn't really surprised that she was there I just had been so focused on fixing things with my dad that I hadn't even thought about the possibility of Latasha being there. I ignored her and spoke to her boys before turning around and walking away from her. I was in no mood for Latasha and her drama, I was already trying to keep my family on one accord with Shakeem being there I didn't need the extra stress. I took my seat at the main table that had been set up in the living room for the adults while the kids sat in the dining room.

"Who was that at door?" My grandmother asked as she placed the mac and cheese on the table. "Tasha and the boys. I think she taking the boys jackets off and stuff." I said, looking over at Shakeem and smiled. "You ok? You enjoying yourself?" I asked him as I grabbed his hand. "Yeah, your brother was just sharing some stories about y'all childhood, you didn't tell me you used to rap." He said with a laugh. I looked over at my brother and rolled my eyes. "Ewww, I can't believe you told him that." I couldn't help but laugh. It felt like the good old days being surrounded by my family and even though my father hadn't said much to me I still felt somewhat at peace.

That is until Latasha started her shit. My mom, unknowingly, started the snowball effect when she asked, "So, Tasha when are you gonna go to Atlanta to spend some time with Moon? I know you need a break from the boys." I was guessing that Latasha hadn't told my mom about our fall out months prior. "Oh, nah Moon be hella busy down there, she don't really have time to be trying to babysit little ole me." She said before scooping up some baked beans and pushing them into her mouth as she looked at me. "Oh please, you guys are best friends I'm sure Moon always has time for you. Right?" My mom asked as I drank some of my sweet tea, seeing as though I had a hard lump forming in my throat. Clearing my throat, I responded, "Tasha never asked to come down there, my house has always been open."

Latasha laughed before responding, "My apologies, what I meant to say was, Moon is too consumed in her own life to even understand what's going on in my life. To be honest, we don't talk much."

"Oh shit." My aunt exclaimed under her breath as her eyes began bouncing between me and Latasha. "Ok, so we doing this?" I asked, throwing my napkin on the table. "Look Tasha, you made the decision to have kids! We had a plan after graduation and you went and got knocked up by the first nigga that gave you the time of day. Every time you call me you always have some type of drama going on and end up borrowing money that you know you'll never be able to repay. I never judged you or turned my back on you but I can't hold your fucking hand!"

"Princess!" My mom blurted out. "My apologies granny, but what we not bout to do is act like I'm just some messed up type of bad friend. I have been here for this girl but I am not her baby daddies." I sat back in my seat and stared at Latasha who had a tear rolling down her face. "Moon you think I give a damn about your money? I vent to you because you were my best friend, but you were too busy taking trips to Barcelona and Dubai to notice your best friend was dying without you here. You think people don't know what happens in Dubai?" She busted into tears but honestly, I wasn't moved. I was feeling good on my Henny and I couldn't have cared less about her theatrics. My mom on the other hand had a soft spot for Latasha and was already on her feet consoling her as I took another sip from my tea. "Moon, maybe you and Tasha should have this conversation in private. You owe her that much, y'all been friends for way too long to be acting like this."

"With all due respect ma, I don't owe anybody a doggone thing. Especially her ungrateful self." My mom shook her head and went to say something else but Latasha cut her off, "No Mrs. Simmons, it's okay, I'm gonna go ahead and leave. It was nice seeing you guys and thank you for having me." Latasha said as she stood from the table and gave them hugs.

My parents were looking at me and shaking their heads but it wasn't my fault that Latasha didn't do anything with her life besides make a couple babies by some broke niggas. Before she walked out of the living room, heading towards the dining room to go get her boys she turned back around and said, "And Moon, I'm really happy for you. I thought your life would've fallen apart after Chanel exposed you for being an escort. Glad that didn't stop you from snagging another baller. I guess you really can turn a hoe into a housewife."

"Ahhh, yeah yeah yeah go get them kids some new shoes." I said loudly. Shakeem and everyone else at the table had stopped eating at this point and were all staring at me. My dad broke the silence when he began speaking, "Princess Marie Simmons, you always find a way to make every interaction all about you. You treat the people that love you like they mean nothing and why? Because they can't give you money and social media fame? Huh? Lord knows I have tried to figure out how you strayed so far from my sweet daughter who used to come to me about everything, who put her family before anything. This woman that you have become I really don't know her. But what I do know is I won't allow you to disrespect your grandmother's home a moment longer." He stood to his feet as he continued, "Shakeem, it was nice meeting you but I'm going to have to ask you all to leave."

"It was nice meeting you all as well and I apologize for everything. Marvin, that's my direct line if you serious about your engineering hit me up next time you in Atlanta." We both stood up as he hugged my grandmother and mother, grabbing my hand and walking me out the front door.

I had knots in my stomach the entire ride back to the hotel. Shakeem was quiet as he swerved through the streets with the music blasting. I knew he was probably thinking so many things in that moment so I left him to his thoughts until we got back to the room.

Upon entering the room Shakeem went straight to the mini bar and downed two of the small shots before turning to me, "So, you used to sell pussy or something?" He asked bluntly as he stared into my eyes, daring me to lie. "Keem, my past doesn't matter. I'm all yours and have been all yours since the day we met. Don't let my broke ass bitter ex best friend try to have you doubting me now." I pleaded as I tried my damnedest to muster up a few tears. I cold see him clenching his teeth as his jaw line tightened, but he remained silent.

This was is, I had to go hard or possibly miss out on securing the bag so you know what my ass did? That's right, I flipped the muthafuckin script on his ass and played right on that soft spot he had for me when I cried. The waterworks were pouring from my eyes as I began, "Baby please don't do this! I love you more than I love myself. I was young and made a few mistakes but I already lost our baby, I can't lose you too! I would die!" I was sobbing into the palms of my hands to keep from laughing.

I couldn't believe the performance I was putting on as he wrapped his arms around me to console me, lifting my head by my chin, and saying, "Shhhhh, come here. A nigga ain't said shit about leaving you. I'm a real nigga I know we all got a past, I just want to know yours so there's no surprises in the future, ya know?"

He rubbed the back of my head while he wiped my tears with his other hand. I knew my guilt trip had worked. I sniffled and dropped my head before asking, "What all do you want to know?" I asked him, trying to stay in character. "Why did your friend mention Dubai?"

**FIND OUT WHAT HAPPENS
NEXT IN:**

**ALL ROADS LEAD TO
DUBAI:**

PROUD HEAUX